OUT IN THE END ZONE

LANE HAYES

For Bob- Under your contagious smile and wacky sense of humor is a brave soul, ready to do battle at a moment's notice. Thank you for being my champion... and my love.

1

"This above all: to thine own self be true."—William Shakespeare, *Hamlet*

THE STEADY BASS of a popular hip-hop song reverberated in the overcrowded living room. The lights had been dimmed to evoke a club-like atmosphere. Partygoers danced on coffee tables and on the patio just outside the open sliding glass doors leading to the backyard. Others bopped to the beat and yelled to be heard above the din. Traversing the sea of inebriated twentysomethings to get to the kitchen would take time, patience, and maybe a raincoat to avoid accidental drink spillage, but it was better than listening to the same stupid stories I'd heard so often I could tell them myself. Why did I think this would be fun?

Oh, right. Because college parties were a blast, I mused sarcastically as my roommate's ex-girlfriend swayed against my side.

I fake laughed on cue, then raised my red cup and signaled I needed more alcohol before making a not-so-stealthy escape. I didn't check to see if I was being followed. I breathed a sigh of relief when I stepped into the kitchen and spotted Chelsea and Mitch.

Chelsea Ramirez was our hostess tonight. She was a petite Latina with a bohemian streak who loved a good time. She didn't think twice about having a hundred people over every other weekend. I met Chelsea through my best friend, Derek, during our sophomore year of college. I'd just switched schools to play football at a small private university in nearby Orange, but I'd made lifelong friends at Long Beach State, like Derek and Chels. I had good friends at Chilton College too—but not like these guys. I didn't mind the sometimes wicked freeway commute. It was more important to me to be close to people who felt like family.

I tapped my empty red cup to Chelsea's, then turned to greet Mitch with a smile that probably looked a tad too enthusiastic. "Hi, there. How's it goin'?" I asked awkwardly.

"It's going well, thank you." He looked amused at my sudden ineptitude. With good reason.

I was a total dweeb around Mitch Peterson.

We met through Chelsea a few years ago, but since we usually only saw each other at parties like this one with a gazillion people around us, I didn't know him well. Truthfully, the guy kind of intimidated me. He had bright blue eyes, short dark-blond hair, and a commanding presence that made him appear taller than he was. I pegged him at five eleven, at least three inches shorter than my own six two. And he was much leaner. No joke, I could bench press him with one hand tied behind my back.

According to Chels, Mitch was a cultural and fashion trend-setter and an active member of a prominent on-campus LGBTQ group. And maybe a cheer captain too? I couldn't remember. He was one of those uber go-getters. You know the type. A 4.0 student, president of multiple clubs...oh yeah, and a budding

YouTube star too. I felt like a slacker in comparison. My grades were decent but after football, my main pastime was hanging out with my friends. No doubt he thought I was a dumb jock.

"Hiding in the kitchen at your own party? You're slipping, Chels," I chided playfully.

Chelsea tossed her dark hair over her shoulder, then rolled her eyes. "Don't go starting rumors, Evan. I have a dilemma, but I'm three kamikazes and two tequila shots into the night, so I'm seeking guidance from my more sober friend 'cause I josh dunno what to do," she slurred.

Uh oh. She was drunk. I supposed that made sense. It was sometime after midnight on a beautiful summer evening in Southern California and the last weekend before school started. A perfect occasion for a party, if one was needed. And Chelsea usually didn't require much persuasion to let loose and have fun. Mitch seemed relatively sober, though I had spotted him dancing on the coffee table with Chelsea when Derek and I first arrived a couple of hours ago.

"What's the problem?" I asked, setting my cup on the counter and reaching for a water bottle.

Mitch shot a guarded look my way. "Sex is happening in her roomie's room."

"Like right this second?" I furrowed my brow and gestured in the general direction of the bedrooms.

"Yup. Rachel doesn't know her room is being used for a slam pad, and Chelsea is having a moment. The way I see it, she has two options." Mitch set a hand on his hip and began a theatrical countdown on the fingers of his free hand. "Option one, she commits coitus interruptus and an embarrassing moment occurs, complete with nudity, animal sounds, and possible screaming. Two, she lets them wrap it up and then kicks their asses to the curb. Which would you choose, Evan? Door number one or door number two?"

"Uh...I need a little clarification before I answer. Animal

sounds *and* screaming? What the fuck are they doing, and who is it? Anyone I know?"

"Jenna and Rory. And what do you think they're doing? They're fucking to their own porny soundtrack...grunting, groaning, 'Oh baby, right there.' You name it, they're doing it. I was about to knock on the door and usher them out, but I'm too close to the situation and once the dialogue started, I just couldn't do it." Mitch sighed, then cocked his head. "But you could."

I pointed at my chest and shook my head emphatically. "No way. I'm not touching that."

Mitch grinned mischievously. "Why not? They might ask you to join them. Isn't that a straight guy's fantasy? Two guys and a girl or is it one guy, two girls or—"

"Not my thing, wise guy. I've had my hands full trying to avoid Amanda for the past hour. She's being very...clingy," I griped.

Chelsea made a funny face. "She's harmless. She's trying to make Derek jealous."

"That's ridiculous. Derek's my best friend. I would never go out with his ex," I huffed.

"That's 'cause you're a good guy, Evan." Chelsea gave me a sappy smile. "Hey, why didn't we ever go out? I guess we still could. We're young and free. But let's not talk about our fushure tonight. I'm a little drunk. I might not remember. And if you and me do somethin', I gotta 'member it."

"Right. Let's get you some water and fresh air," Mitch said, handing her a water bottle.

"First, I gotta fix the happy humper situation."

"I'll take care of it." Mitch gently guided her outside through the kitchen door.

"You can't. Rory is your—"

"Don't worry, Chels. I won't go by myself," Mitch turned to me with a look I couldn't quite read. "Evan will help me. Right, Evan?"

"Uh..."

"See? He's brimming with enthusiasm! God, I love that in a guy," he teased.

I snickered at his comedic expression and uncapped my bottle of water. I guzzled half of it, then looked up to find Mitch paused in the doorway, giving me an admiring double take. He did that sometimes. Maybe it was his way of testing my "straight dude" boundaries. The thought alone should have made me chuckle. Gay or straight or anywhere in between...a little flirting never hurt anyone. But when my heart did a funny flip in my chest that left me feeling dizzy, I wondered for the umpteenth time why I didn't seem immune to him.

I followed them outdoors and sucked in a breath of balmy evening air. It was a gorgeous night, and the relative quiet was a nice change from the chaotic atmosphere of the house. I stood next to Mitch and surveyed the yard. Light spilled from the living room onto the deck, but the shadows were long and it was hard to see well. I spotted Derek sitting on the top step of the deck, chatting with a few people I didn't recognize. I sipped my water and cast a sideways glance at Mitch and Chelsea as they greeted a few friends on the lawn.

I hung back and started to turn away just as Mitch glanced over his shoulder.

"You look lost in thought. Are you planning your getaway?" Mitch asked.

"Getaway from what?"

"Me."

"No, I...uh..." I tried to think of a witty reply and came up with, "How's school going?"

Fuck. See? What the hell was wrong with me? I couldn't open my mouth without saying something lame around him.

Mitch's crooked smile made his eyes light up, which was a funny thing to notice in the dark. It made him look...pretty. Or maybe that was the wrong word. Compelling fit better. And interesting. He looked like the type of person who always had twenty balls in the air and a million thoughts in his head. Yet somehow, he seemed perfectly in control.

"Well, it hasn't started yet, but my classes look interesting this semester. You?"

"Same. We start next week."

Silence.

That was my cue. I nodded distractedly and stepped backward, mentally preparing my exit speech. Then I opened my mouth and spewed more awkwardness.

"Do you live here with Chelsea now?" I knew the answer but apparently, I was determined to up my lame game.

"Me? Here? Are you insane?" He shuddered dramatically.

"What's wrong with it?" I asked, glancing around the darkened yard of our friend's notorious party pad.

"Nothing at all...unless you like waking up with strangers on your sofa."

"Or screwing in your bed," I interjected with a half laugh.

A shadow crossed his face, making him look impossibly sad. Before I could ask what was wrong, he smiled and the frown faded so fast I could have convinced myself I'd imagined it.

"I love Chelsea and I'd do almost anything for her, but I need peace and quiet too. Like right now...this is nice. People are talking and you can hear the music through the open door, but it's a welcoming background noise layered with silence."

"I don't hear silence," I countered as someone howled with laughter.

"Compared to inside, it's ghostly quiet."

"True. So where do you live? You've probably told me but I forgot," I asked conversationally.

"A few blocks away in the studio apartment above my grandmother's garage. How's that for swanky?"

"Super swanky."

He chuckled and there it was again. That extra twinkle or spark or something. I tilted my head to get a better look at him. Mitch was a good-looking guy with sharp, angular features, chiseled cheekbones, a square jaw, and a straight nose. And he was fit and toned like a gymnast. Which made sense since he was a cheer...person.

"Are you a cheerleader still?" I blurted.

Mitch narrowed his gaze slightly. "You are all over the map tonight."

"Sorry. That was random," I acknowledged with a self-deprecating shrug. "Is cheerleader the right word, or is it cheer person or—"

"I suppose either works and yes, I'm on the squad this year. It's my last hurrah, so I'll have to enjoy every second I can ogling sexy men in uniform," he said with a dreamy sigh. "I'm assuming football players are equally pervy about the cheer squad at your school. And vice versa. All those hunky boys in tight tights checking out the girls...and the guys."

"I don't know about that."

Mitch scoffed. "I doubt everyone on your team is straight. Chances are beyond high there are at least a couple of queers. It's the one-in-ten law of nature. Don't bother refuting it."

I raised a brow. "I'm not arguing, man. You're probably right. No one is out that I know of, but it's not my business either way. Love is love."

Mitch fixed me with a thoughtful stare, then nodded slowly. "Yes. That's true."

The quiet unnerved me after a few moments. I gestured toward the house. "We aren't really kicking anyone out of the bedroom, are we?"

"I'm doing my best to avoid it. Yes, it's incredibly tacky to fuck on someone else's bed during a party, but people do it all the time. The problem is, they've been in there for a while."

"Why didn't Chelsea bang on the door?"

"She did, but Rory is—it's not that easy. It's sort of a dual screw thing. A physical action and a personal 'fuck you,' " he explained cryptically.

"Chelsea and Rory?" I asked, furrowing my brow.

"No." He glanced over at our hostess, who'd been enveloped into a larger group of friends standing nearby. "Let's change the subject. What were we talking about? Closeted athletes? You know, I've had at least three boyfriends in college who started out so deep in the closet, they were practically in Narnia. *The Chronicles of Narnia* and don't tell me you've never read them."

"*The Lion, the Witch and the Wardrobe*, right?"

He beamed and nodded. "Yes, and six other books. All of them so wonderful!"

"Now *I'm* confused. Are we talking about closets, athletes, sex, or books?"

Mitch snorted. "If I have a choice, I'd rather talk about sex than books."

I shot him an amused sideways glance, then chugged the last of my water and squashed the bottle in one hand like a piece of paper. His gaze shifted from my hand to my eyes and this time, I felt a corresponding tug in my groin. No joke. My dick actually twitched against the zipper of my Levi's. This was what happened when someone brought up sex. Okay, so I was the one who brought it up—but still.

"Everything comes back to sex," I said sagely.

He did that arched-brow trick again and gave me a shrewd once-over. "Is that so?"

"Oh, hell yes. Humans have sex on the brain all the fucking time. If we're not doing it, we're talking about it or watching it. There are actual studies averaging the hours we think about sex every day."

"Hours? Come on. Are you that big of a horndog?"

I squinted as though mulling his question seriously, then nodded. "Well, yeah. I guess I am. You probably are too."

"True. I am."

"See? Derek Googled it once. Men think about sex every seven seconds. *Boom!* You just thought about it. Admit it."

Mitch grinned. "Guilty."

I held up my hand for a high five and chuckled. "So...what sexy thing were you thinking about?"

"This conversation has taken an interesting turn," he commented sarcastically. "Fine. I'll give you a hint. A blowjob, a hand job, a rim job, or just plain ol' screwing. Take your pick."

I narrowed my gaze and teasingly asked, "What's rimming, again?"

"Google it," he suggested innocently.

I held eye contact as I pulled my cell from my back pocket. "Siri, what is rimming?"

"I'm sorry. I didn't understand. Would you repeat that, please?"

Mitch busted up laughing. "You can't ask Siri. You'll be there all day."

"Then why don't you just tell me?"

"It's anal oral sex, genius."

"Oh." I let the visual take shape in my head as I slipped my cell into my pocket and clandestinely adjusted my cock. "Got it. And that feels good?"

"Ah-mazing. You should try it sometime." He winked, then took another sip of water.

"What makes you think I haven't? Just 'cause I didn't know the terminology doesn't mean I'm not an expert."

"I think that's exactly what it means," he quipped. "And even if you were an expert at giving...which I doubt, I highly recommend being on the receiving end. If your partner knows what he's doing, it can be better than a blowjob."

"Nothing's better than a blowjob." I snorted derisively.

"Anal is better. In my opinion, anyway."

"Hmm. We should probably switch topics," I remarked with a frown.

Mitch snickered. "Sorry. I should have warned you sex is my

favorite subject. If you aren't careful, you'll end up hearing more than you ever wanted to know about the joys of gay sex."

"I don't mind. Sex is sex."

"Ahh. Right. And love is love," he said, throwing my earlier words back at me.

"Sure. As long as it's respectful, consensual, and everyone leaves feeling good, what difference does it make if you're gay, straight, or somewhere in between? Sexuality is fluid."

"Are you bi?" he asked slowly as though mulling over the possibility.

"Maybe. I'm just me," I said in a cavalier tone. I greeted an old acquaintance passing by with a fist bump before turning back to my befuddled looking companion. "What's wrong?"

"Nothing. You just might be perfect for..."

"For what?"

"Um...nothing. Would you classify yourself as curious?" he asked intently.

"Classify? That sounds kinda scientific. Let's just say I've gone through shit in my life that's made me realize it's best to be open to possibility. I might live to be a hundred, or I might die tomorrow. Choose love, choose happiness, and choose your own truth."

My phone buzzed in my pocket. I pulled it out and glanced at the message from Derek. *Are you ready?* To leave? Now? Hell no. I hadn't been this interested in a conversation at a party in eons. I wasn't going anywhere. I shoved it into my back pocket without replying.

"You really feel that way?" Mitch asked.

"Of course."

"Oh, my God. I think this is fate. You'd be perfect for my senior project." Mitch's eyes lit up excitedly. He stepped back and gave me a thorough once-over, then paused abruptly. "Unless...do you have a girlfriend?"

"No. Why?"

"It wouldn't work if you were attached," he said, resting his elbow on one hand as he scratched his chin thoughtfully.

"Oh. Do you have a boyfriend?"

"No, but that doesn't matter."

"Why not?"

"I'd rather not say. I have to think about this. I haven't had much to drink tonight, but I don't want to make a rash party *faux pas* and ask you something I might regret in the morning."

"Oh, like 'What do you think about rim jobs?' "

"Ha. Ha. You brought up sex. Not me," he insisted with a laugh before brushing a stray piece of hair behind his ear.

I observed the elegant bend of his wrist in a weird daze for a moment and snapped out of it when my phone buzzed in my pocket again. I pulled it out and read the second message from Derek asking if I was ready to go.

I glanced up and spotted my best friend sitting on the deck, nursing a bottle of water. Derek Vaughn looked like a typical California kid. He was a six-foot-two water polo player with dark blond hair, blue eyes, and a toned swimmer's physique. In a way, it was funny we'd become good friends. We were total opposites. He was an uptight, neat freak and an overachiever. I was...not. And other than being the same height, we were nothing alike in the looks department either. I had brown hair, brown eyes, and a thicker, more muscular build. I outweighed him by at least forty pounds.

I bet he was outside killing time and trying to steer clear of Amanda. I felt a twinge of sympathy, but it wasn't strong enough to pull me away from Mitch. Derek was a big boy. He could get himself home. I caught his eye and shook my head irritably, then put my cell away just as one of Amanda's friends sidled up next to me and slipped her hand under my shirt.

"Hey, Evan," she said in a breathy voice before turning to Mitch. "Chelsea says someone heard the lovebirds fighting and wondered if you'd talked to Rory yet."

"Fuck," Mitch sighed, pushing his hand through his perfectly coiffed hair. "I better deal with this. I'll see you, Ev—"

"I'll come with you." Mitch and the girl, whose name I should have probably known but didn't, both shot dumbfounded looks my way. "What? You said you needed help."

Mitch held my gaze before gesturing for me to follow him into the house. The decibel level rose the second we crossed the threshold. We made our way through the mass of sweaty partiers in the living room and then down a long, narrow hallway covered in concert posters. He stopped in front of the last door on the right and leaned in as though listening for any telltale noises before knocking.

I set my hand on the doorjamb and assumed a badass bouncer pose. Truthfully, I had no idea what I was doing now. I had zero interest in rustling lovers out of a borrowed bedroom, but it seemed almost cowardly to let Mitch deal with Chelsea's badly behaved guests alone. This wasn't his fight either.

Okay, fine. The truth was I didn't want to leave him. Not until he told me more about his mystery project. I wanted all the titillating details, I mused, glancing backward when someone bumped my shoulder.

Fuck. Not again.

"Hey, Evan. Are you sure you want to go in there? They're a bit preoccupied." Amanda gave me a pretty pouty look I might have found interesting under other circumstances. Like A—if she wasn't Derek's ex and B—if she wasn't interfering with whatever adventure I'd embarked on with Mitch.

"So I heard. Well...I didn't actually hear but everyone else did," I clarified.

Mitch rolled his eyes and knocked again. "Rory? Rory, it's me."

The knob twisted and then the door slowly inched open. A bare-chested, tattooed muscleman I assumed was Rory stepped into the light. "What are you doing here?"

He reminded me of a military badass with his camo-print

pants, super short brown hair, and copious ink. He was my height but more muscular. I didn't think I'd ever met Rory, but Mitch obviously knew him well. There was something in the way they looked at each other that was very...familiar.

Mitch lowered his voice when he spoke. "You have to leave."

Amanda tugged at my elbow and gave me a meaningful look and hooked her thumb. "We should go too," she whispered.

No way. I wasn't going anywhere. I was too fascinated by the silent conversation happening between Rory and Mitch. It was weird as fuck and very interesting. Were they lovers?

The door flung open and a wild-eyed brunette with smeared mascara and red lipstick stormed into the hallway. She wore an unbuttoned red plaid men's shirt that exposed her lacy black bra over her short, tight jean skirt. And she held a pair of high heels in one hand like a weapon. Next to the half-dressed man, it was easy to piece together the story. There was a fight, angry sex, and now...I had no clue. But I wanted to grab a chair and some popcorn and see what happened next. And I wanted to be sure Mitch was okay. The air was tense and unfriendly.

She bared her teeth and growled menacingly. "Oh, my God, Rory! I should have known. You just wanted to make him jealous, didn't you? I hate you. Stay away from me, asshole!"

"Jenna, stop!" Rory yelled.

My football training kicked in. I operated on instinct. Protect and shield. Of course, my job on the field was to protect the quarterback and keep the ball safe, but I supposed the same applied to an angry woman making a break from the guy who'd pissed her off. I stepped in front of Rory, barring his way, then motioned for Amanda to go after Jenna.

"Leave her alone," I said sharply.

"Who are you?" Before I could respond, Rory turned to Mitch with a frown. "Are you fucking this guy?"

"Yes," I growled a half beat before Mitch said, "No."

Mitch gaped at me in surprise, then stepped between us. He

spoke in a voice so low, I wouldn't have heard if I wasn't standing a foot away. "Why are you doing this? It's over. You know it."

"No," Rory whispered. "I miss you. I...please just—"

"Stop. Just...go home. Please," Mitch replied sadly.

The ensuing standoff was intense. Especially for an outsider desperately trying to figure out what was going on.

"I don't have my truck," Rory said before rounding on me. "Who is he? He's not good enough for you. He's not going treat you right. I can tell and I—"

"I'll call a ride for you," Mitch replied before turning to me. "Would you mind making sure Jenna gets home okay? I know she's with Amanda but—"

"Are you sure?" I stepped backward when he nodded, intending to launch into action but I stopped in my tracks. "Don't disappear. I want to talk to you...babe."

Mitch narrowed his gaze at the unexpected endearment, then inclined his head and turned away.

Fuck, this was strange. They didn't go together at all. Mitch was willowy and elegant and vaguely effeminate while Rory was a muscle-bound meathead. He looked like the kind of guy who picked fights in bars for kicks. Or a schoolyard bully. Nope. I couldn't see it. Or maybe I just didn't like it.

I paused at the end of the hallway and glanced back at them. And immediately wished I hadn't. Mitch held Rory's hands while the bigger man bent his head in what looked like regret. They appeared to be deep in conversation, and I could only imagine it was one of those painful "it's really over" chats. I should have walked away, but something rooted me to the spot. Yes, I was stuck on the incongruity of them as a couple, but I was also drawn to the emotion between them. It felt heavy...but real. Their connection fascinated me. It allowed me to let go of the physical differences and witness an intimacy that frankly made me...jealous.

I pushed that thought aside and hurried outside. I spotted

Amanda and Jenna on the street in front of the passenger side of an idling Honda Civic. Amanda gestured for the other girl to get into the car; then she shut the door before turning toward the house. I met her on the sidewalk with my hands stuffed in my pockets.

"Is she okay?" I asked.

"She'll be fine after she gets through the mega hangover coming her way in the morning. I wonder if those two were on something. One minute they were all over each other and the next..." Amanda pursed her red lips and sighed. "Honestly, they made me glad I'm single again."

"Hmm." I wasn't going to engage in any conversation about her breakup with Derek. I tried to think of a polar segue and came up blank.

"Are you seeing anyone?" she asked.

"No," I replied.

I was relieved when I caught sight of Mitch and Rory moving down the pathway in my periphery. Mitch gave me a subtle nod of acknowledgment I clung to like a lifeline. I read it as a "Thanks for helping," and "I'll be there in a sec," instead of the good-bye it might have been. I watched Rory head toward a waiting Prius and breathed a silent sigh of relief when Mitch didn't hop in with him.

Amanda turned to see what I was looking at and shook her head in wonder. "I had no idea they were a couple until tonight. Did you?"

"No, but I just met them. I mean...I just met Rory and Jenna. I know Mitch," I said awkwardly.

"Hmm. People aren't always what they seem. Rory, Gabe..." She gestured toward the handsome water polo player heading down the sidewalk. "I heard he's gay too."

"Gabe? I don't think so." Of course, I didn't know anything about the guy except that he was a new addition to Derek's water polo team. I wasn't sure why she'd bring that up or—

"You're cute, Evan," Amanda purred, running a manicured fingernail down the row of buttons on my shirt.

Fuck. This was exactly what I'd hoped to avoid. The seductive cadence in her voice freaked me out. Could this night get any stranger?

I gently removed her hand. "Look, Amanda, I'm not—"

She set a finger on my lips and shook her head. She was so close now; I could smell her perfume and see the glint of desire in her blue eyes. Amanda was a sexy woman by anyone's standards. She had long blonde hair, a flawless sense of style, and an edginess that appealed to most guys. But I didn't trust her or particularly like her, and I'd always thought the feeling was mutual. In June, when Derek told me they broke up, I'd been secretly relieved for his sake. Just like Mitch and Rory, Derek didn't belong with Amanda.

"Shh. I know what you're thinking, but you're wrong. I have a friend who's been trying to meet you for a while."

"Huh?" Okay. That was unexpected.

"Her name is Nicole," she continued quickly when she spotted Mitch walking toward us. "She goes to Chilton with you and maybe—"

"Well, that's a relief! Is Jenna on her way home too?" Mitch asked, bumping my elbow.

"She is," Amanda replied before turning to me. "I'll see you inside, Ev. I want to make sure I give you Nicole's number."

Mitch and I stared after Amanda as she moved toward the house, then looked at each other with matching wide-eyed expressions before cracking up.

But I still had to ask, "What the hell was that all about?"

"If you mean Rory, it's complicated."

"I bet. Let me see if I can put it together." I furrowed my brow and tapped my finger on my chin thoughtfully. "Your jealous ex was trying to make you jealous?"

"Seems like it," he said tiredly before adding, "Kind of like what Amanda was doing with you and Derek."

"She actually just told me wants to set me up with a friend of hers, who I'm pretty sure I already know. In fact, I'm missing her party to be at this one."

"It seems so convoluted. You'd think these stupid games would get old by now. We're all in our twenties. Why do some of us still act like such idiots?"

I had no answer for that one, so I left it alone. "How old are you?"

"Twenty-three. You?"

"Same."

Silence.

"Were you *with* that guy?" I asked, unable to keep the confusion from my voice.

"Yeah. For a year. We broke up for the last time two months ago. It looks like Jenna is my replacement," he said matter-of-factly. "And now Rory thinks you're his replacement. That was funny. Thanks for jumping in to defend me. I appreciate it."

"You're welcome." I bit my bottom lip before continuing. "What did you see in him? He just doesn't look like your type."

"What's my type?" Mitch asked with a laugh.

"Someone nicer who's...more like you." I winced the second the words left my mouth. Awkward.

"Thanks, I think. But Rory is actually very nice. And smart too. He's also a little tortured. A closeted hunky athlete battling self-worth and questioning his sexuality. What can I say? I have a gay fairy godmother complex. Don't say I didn't warn you." Mitch sighed in defeat and pulled his phone from his back pocket. "Hey, give me your number. If you're still interested, we can talk about my project next week when you're free. No pressure. If you don't return my text, I'll understand."

I recited my number, noting the graceful bend of his head as his fingers flew over the tiny keyboard on his cell.

"What's this project about?" I asked.

"I'll tell you when we meet. My mind is all over the place right now. I'm entering my personal witching hour." He chuckled at my perplexed expression before explaining. "Basically, it's that pivotal moment in every fairy tale when the clock strikes midnight and the hero or heroine is about to be left in rags with a useless glass slipper and a wild story no one will believe."

"Hopefully you have some cool mouse friends to keep you company in your dungeon until Prince Charming comes back with your shoe," I said with a laugh.

Mitch snorted derisively. "Disney princesses are confined to towers, Evan. Not dungeons. And if I find any rodents in my apartment, I'm not making friends. I'm calling an exterminator. Ciao!"

"Hang on. Are you ditching me?" I closed the distance between us and fixed him with a mock glare.

"Of course not but...why do you want to hang out with me? Amanda wants to introduce you to her friends and—"

"And I like being with you. Your ex thinks we're a new couple, and he might not be here, but people talk. Why not give him a taste of his own medicine?"

"And have sex in someone's else's bedroom?" he deadpanned.

I grinned and shook my head. "Not my kink."

Mitch threw his head back and laughed. The joyful sound had a pretty ring to it that made me wish I had something clever to add. "It's not mine either. But beware, Evan. You're tall, dark, and handsome, and I really don't feel like being on my best behavior anymore. It's not personal. It's just me."

"I'll take my chances."

He regarded me thoughtfully and nodded. "Okay. But if you don't mind...I don't want to talk about Rory or his maybe-girl-friend. And I don't want to talk about sex. Or anything that's fairly simple but sometimes gets complicated. So don't ask me about my project or—"

"Wait. Is this a sex project?" I asked, widening my eyes comically.

Mitch snorted. "I wish. All I'm saying is that I really want to slip into neutral and think about stupid, shallow things like... when are they releasing the lineup for Coachella?"

"Headliner...Justin Timberlake." I spread my hands wide and nodded like I knew what I was talking about.

"Really? Hmm. I was hoping it would be Britney, but she has Vegas," he said in a faraway tone.

"Maybe Drake."

Mitch furrowed his brow and gave me a sharp look. "You have no clue, do you?"

"None."

"Hilarious," he scoffed. "I bet it'll be..."

I followed Mitch back into the house to hang out at a party I no longer cared about just to talk to him. I hadn't felt this way around a guy in almost five years. I didn't ask myself why. That wasn't my style. I was a firm believer that if it felt good, I should do it. And hanging out on the back deck, staring up at the summer stars while dissecting our favorite bands, breakfast cereals, and cocktail recipes as the party fizzled around us was, oddly enough, exactly what I wanted to do.

All night long.

2

Sunday morning came way too soon. I heard Derek shuffle down the hall at nine o'clock and briefly wondered why the fuck he was up so early before pulling my pillow over my head and falling back asleep till noon. I stretched my arms above my head and rubbed my eyes, then reached for my cell to check messages. The first one to pop was from an unknown number. And it was very...chatty.

Hi Evan. This is Mitch. Did we say coffee or lunch or drinks? I have practice every morning this week, and I bet you do too. I'm free any time after one, except for Tuesday and Thursday. I work late those days, but any other day should be okay. Let me know what you think. If you don't respond, I won't be offended. But it would be rude, so you should probably at least return my text and let me know if you're still interested. Okay? Have a good day!

I read the message twice before replying.

You've committed a series of texting crimes. Free tomorrow at 1. Lunch at Grub Hub?

Grub Hub? No thanks. Let's meet at The Grill. And what texting crimes?

I chuckled at his green-faced grossed-out emoji, salad bowl, and five question marks, then typed, *I'll tell you tomorrow.*

I stared at his single heart response longer than necessary before making myself get out of bed. There was football on TV and a fridge full of food. My day was set.

TELEVISED preseason pro football wasn't always the most entertaining. Teams were tweaking their lineups and testing the readiness of their rookie players before the games counted. I didn't mind. Football was football and I freaking loved it. I always had. I lived and breathed the game from an early age. My childhood room was still decked with pennants, framed jerseys, and prized footballs I'd collected in my youth. As a kid, I couldn't get enough of the Green Bay Packers and Brett Favre. Don't judge. I was six at the time, and they were the fucking bomb. Hell, I still loved them.

LA didn't have a football team back then. The closest live football involved a two and a half hour drive to San Diego. My dad took my brother, Eli, and me one year to see the Chargers play my beloved Packers and it changed my life. Okay...maybe it didn't change anything, but it opened a world of possibility that solidified into a real dream when my dad told me that if I worked hard, there was no reason I couldn't become the world's best football player one day too.

Life hadn't exactly gone according to plan. Playing four years of football at a Division Three private university wasn't my ticket to the NFL. The realization that my original dream might not come true had been a hard pill to swallow at first, but I'd adjusted pretty well—if I did say so myself. I lived a couple of blocks from the ocean with my best friend in a sweet bungalow his parents bought after we moved out of the dorms at Long Beach State. They didn't want Derek living just anywhere or with any ol' roommate. Maybe they were a touch overbearing and controlling, but the rent was free at their insistence, so I sure as hell wouldn't complain.

I had the best of both worlds. I lived in Long Beach and in my spare time, I hung out with the group of friends I'd met during my freshman year. And I played football and went to Chilton College twenty minutes away in Orange with a whole other set of friends. Not bad for a guy who'd been knocking on death's door his senior year of high school. I had a lot to be grateful for, I mused as Derek walked into the living room.

He bumped my fist in greeting, then flopped onto the armchair next to the sofa in a pose that should have come across as uber relaxed. Unfortunately, the tension radiating from him killed the vibe. Derek was a world-class worrier. I had no idea who'd pissed in his Cheerios, but he'd tell me in his own time. And if you asked me, that was why we were best friends. I was mostly mellow and laid-back while Derek was uptight and fastidious. But we respected boundaries and complemented each other. I encouraged him to have fun and not take life so seriously, and he encouraged me to stay focused and pick up my shit around the house. *Win-win.*

"Where've you been?" I asked.

"Coffee with Chelsea. I think that's all the activity I can stand today. My head hurts and my stomach is off."

"Ah. A good ol' fashioned hangover. No wonder you look like shit." I waited for his scowl before adding, "It's not like you to get wasted."

"Don't remind me. I need greasy pizza or a burrito to sop up the excess alcohol in my system." He groaned. "What time did you get home?"

"I dunno. Three, I think."

"Three?" he repeated. "What was happening at three? Probably nothing good, so tell me all about it."

I gave a half laugh and shrugged. "Nothing really. I hung out with Mitch most of the night."

"Mitch?"

"Why are you repeating everything I say?" I frowned. "Yes. Mitch."

"Hmm. What would you and Mitch possibly have to talk about until three a.m.?"

"Music, school...random stuff."

I gave him a brief breakdown of the Rory and Jenna sideshow. Then I told him about Amanda's overtures and my theory that she wanted to make him jealous. Derek scoffed distractedly but seemed a bit agitated when I mentioned that she'd also claimed to know that his new teammate was gay. He went quiet for a bit before leaning forward and giving me a sideways glance.

"You know Rory and Mitch were a couple, right?" he asked.

"I found out last night, but...how did you know?"

"Chelsea. She knows everything," he reminded me.

"Oh. Yeah." I frowned and once again gave my full attention to the action on the flat-screen.

"Mitch is a good guy. You'd make a cute couple," he teased.

"Gee, thanks." I batted my eyelashes and clandestinely pulled a throw pillow over my crotch. I didn't know what my deal was, but just talking about Mitch made my dick swell. I had to change the topic quickly. "Are you hungry?"

Derek jumped out of his chair and held his phone up. "Yeah. I've never needed french fries more in my life. Are you in?"

"Yeah, but only if we get Del Taco. I want a burrito, nachos, a quesadilla...one of everything. Real life starts tomorrow. I have practice at six, class at nine, and then I have to be here for lunch before heading back to Orange for—"

"Why would you come home for lunch? You hate commuting."

Oops. I'd said too much. I gave him a blank stare and pointed at his cell. "Dentist appointment. You can't order Del Taco on your phone, dumbshit. You gotta drive."

He groaned pathetically. "Oh, no. I can't drive. I'm much too hungover. Rock, paper, scissors?"

I chuckled but nodded in agreement, thankful for the silly diversion. I loved Derek like a second brother and I trusted him for sure, but I didn't want to talk about Mitch at all. Our wacky, all-over-the-map conversations from the night before and our upcoming lunch were a bit of a mystery to me too. I couldn't explain why I'd agreed to meet him in the middle of a busy Monday. But the truth was...I couldn't wait.

THE LOCKER ROOM was stifling hot after practice Monday morning. We had state-of-the-art amenities, like a high ceiling, bigger than average individual lockers, and amazing water pressure in the showers. And not to brag, but we even had a sauna and Jacuzzi. Private school perks were awesome, but they couldn't make up for the unseasonably warm weather outside and the intense workout we'd just had on the field. My body ached all over. I wanted nothing more than to take advantage of the Jacuzzi, then go home and take a three-hour nap. Not happening. I had twenty minutes to get to class before heading to Long Beach.

I figured out the timing in my head. If I left Orange at noon, I could be in Long Beach within half an hour if traffic cooperated. Maybe I'd swing by the house and—

"Yo, di Angelo! Where were you this weekend? You missed Nicole's party. It's cool, man. I kept her company."

I slipped my short-sleeved shirt over my shoulders and tossed a blank look at Jonesie. He was a beast of a guy. Six foot six, two hundred and ninety pounds of sheer muscle. Well, maybe a little fat too. Jonesie loved his Oreos. And he loved a good time. He always knew where to find the best parties, which in his mind were the ones with the hottest babes who treated football players like rock stars or God's gift to mankind.

Star treatment was a powerful aphrodisiac, but it wasn't my thing. Been there, done that. I'd rather have a two-way conversation with someone based on common interests than soak up mindless admiration and hope it led to getting laid. And waking up next to a stranger whose name I couldn't remember lost its appeal the first time I'd done it. But Jonesie, whose first name I'd forgotten the day he told me, was a couple of years younger than me. He wasn't ready to hang up his party hat anytime soon.

"I bet. Did you have fun?" I asked.

"Can't remember, so yeah, it was probably awesome. Nicole was looking for you, though. She was real disappointed you didn't show up. I told her you'd be around this weekend." He waggled his thick brows lasciviously and slapped high fives with a couple of the guys getting ready nearby.

"How do you know I'm gonna be around this weekend? I'm a busy man, Jonesie." I tied my shoes as fast as possible. Then I swung my workout bag over my shoulder and started buttoning my shirt.

"We've got a game, man. You gotta hang with us afterward."

"Right." I flashed my best noncommittal smile and bumped his arm as I made my way to the exit.

"If you don't want her, I call dibs," he shouted.

I stopped in my tracks and scowled as I turned around. I wanted to smack the shit-eating, pompous look off his face, but I literally didn't have time to get into a fight. However, I wasn't going to let him off the hook.

"Don't talk like that, dude. She's a person, not a fucking ice cream flavor. Show some respect and show some fuckin' class," I huffed derisively.

All eyes were on us for a second or two before the silence was interrupted by a flood of idiotic hoots and catcalls. I held eye contact with him for half a beat longer, then walked away.

The unexpected surge of adrenaline propelled me across campus in record time. I had no regrets about telling Jonesie off, but I was pissed that he'd opened his mouth in front of an audience because I knew how this shit worked. He'd apologize at our next practice...after he made sure Nicole knew I'd stood up for her, which in his mind meant I was hot for the gorgeous brunette who'd been stalking me off and on all summer. He'd make it sound like a sleazy but honest infatuation with a chance of something more. *Fuck.* This was the stuff that made me grateful I was graduating next May.

THE GRILL WAS LOCATED in Belmont Shores. The vibe in this section of Long Beach varied from bohemian chic to family-oriented but still hip. I found a parking spot on the street a block away from the restaurant and lucked out again when the hostess led me to an outdoor table for two under a big yellow umbrella. I thanked her, then pulled my sunglasses out of my front pocket and sat back in my chair to partake in some first-class people-watching until Mitch arrived.

The posse of stylish young moms decked in yoga gear pushing strollers, the older woman walking her ginormous French poodle with a bright pink bow tied around her collar. Nothing outlandish today. I opened my menu and fumbled it a moment later when someone tapped my shoulder.

"Hi, there! Sorry I'm late."

Mitch pulled out the chair across from me and smiled. Damn, he had a nice smile. It was kind of toothy and made his eyes crinkle at the corners and then light up with a sincerity that took my breath away. Most people didn't smile like that. They guardedly gave you pieces of themselves they thought you wanted instead of just being real.

"No prob. How's your day goin'?" I stared at the menu unseeing, hoping to get my suddenly erratic heartbeat under control.

"Busy. I had practice early this morning and I didn't sleep very well, so—" He glanced up when a good-looking waiter stopped by our table to introduce himself and take our drink orders. "I'm fine with water, thank you. And I'm ready to order if you are, Evan."

"Uh...sure. Go ahead."

"I'll have the spinach salad, dressing on the side, hold the bacon and double the avocado. Oh! And can we get a side of fries, please?"

The waiter's indulgent grin dimmed slightly when he turned to take my order. "I'll have the burger and I'll take the bacon my friend is leaving off his salad, and we don't want a side of fries. We need a plate. Or a platter. The bigger, the better. I'm starving."

"Got it. What would you like to drink?" the waiter asked.

"Do you have chocolate milk?"

"We should be able to do that. We have milk and there's chocolate syrup for sundaes so...sure. Anything else?" The waiter addressed both of us, but his gaze roamed back to Mitch, who shook his head and thanked him again.

"He has a crush on you," I commented when we were alone again. "I betcha I wouldn't get chocolate milk if it wasn't for you, so cheers."

Mitch raised his water glass and tapped it against mine. "Hmm. Two questions. One, what makes you think he has a crush on me? And two, who over the age of ten orders chocolate milk with a burger? Ew."

I snickered at his "yuck" face and gave him a lopsided pirate's smile. "Me. And don't look now, but our waiter is checkin' you out again."

Mitch cast a sideways glance at the waiter and gave me a Cheshire cat grin. "He *is* cute. Should I give him my number?"

I shrugged nonchalantly, though the idea bugged the hell out of me. "I dunno. That's your business. My business is finding out important shit like...what do you have against chocolate milk?"

He chuckled as he pulled his sunglasses from his shirt pocket and set them on his nose. "Nothing in particular. I've read all the studies about how the balance of protein and carbohydrates make it an ideal post-workout drink, but I don't like it. I haven't had chocolate milk in a decade. I'd rather have a protein shake."

I creased my forehead in *faux* confusion, then lowered my sunglasses and gave him a knowing look as I pumped my fist suggestively. "Oh. You mean like..."

"Get your mind out of the gutter," he said primly.

I laughed and once I started, I couldn't stop. Mitch kicked me under the table and then leaned across to smack my hand. He rolled his eyes when I shook my hand as if in pain. Then he dipped his fingers into my water and flicked it at me.

"Hey!"

"Don't even think about retaliating," he warned when I reached for my glass.

"You can't just tell me not to do it. You have to call a truce," I said. "It's a rule. Like in football. If you step out of bounds, the play is dead. Not because I told you so but because it's been discussed and agreed upon by all parties before being written down. No one gets to run willy-nilly up and down the field to get to the end zone."

"Fine. We'd better call a truce because if you get my new shirt wet, I may go ballistic."

"I like it. You look nice." I gave the light blue button-down garment a once-over and tried not to stare at the hint of skin at his open collar. It was kind of...sexy.

"Thank you. I bought it yesterday. I had a much-needed retail therapy session I may regret when I get my next credit card statement, but it felt good at the time. Maybe even necessary after that episode with Rory Saturday night. We don't need to go over all of it again, but...thank you for being there and for being so cool. I know it was weird. I was afraid you might not want to meet me today."

"Nah." I waved dismissively. "The part with Rory was unexpected, but the rest was really...nice."

"Yeah. I think a few of our friends were talking about us the next day," he said cagily.

"What'd they say?"

He gave me a crooked smile. "The usual 'Mitch has a crush on a straight boy' kind of thing. I hoped I didn't scare you away."

"I don't scare easily, and I'm too curious about your mystery project. Tell me all about it."

Mitch took a sip of water, then cleared his throat theatrically but still didn't speak for a few moments. "Okay...well, um."

"Not a good start," I teased.

Mitch snickered. "I know. Sorry. I'm nervous and I don't know why. All right, let me try again. I'm a communications major. My senior project is a thesis exploring the impact of social media, specifically in video format."

"Like on YouTube?"

"Yes, exactly. I think there's a strong argument that reality television and now platforms like Instagram and Twitter are popular because they give every regular guy and gal their instant fifteen minutes of fame. But they're better because the fame stretches with every 'like' and comment on their pages. We eat up details in other people's lives with more interest than our own. Have you noticed how many 'couples' have their own YouTube channels? Some of them make bank too."

"How?" I asked incredulously.

"Sponsorships. Businesses advertise with YouTube sensations with lots of subscribers. They know thousands of people tune in to watch snippets of a cute couple making an impromptu dinner. Viewers fawn over how attentive and sweet they are to each other. The way one guy rubs his boyfriend's back while he stirs marinara sauce and then—"

"Are we talking about gay couples?"

"Of course. I mean, it's all out there. Gay, straight, bi, trans, pansexual...one partner, two....But I try to stick with what I know. And I know I'm gay," Mitch announced.

I smiled at the server who stopped by the table at that moment to deliver our lunches. When he stepped aside, I grabbed a few french fries and popped them into my mouth.

"You don't say?" I snarked.

"That's not going to be a problem for you, is it?"

"Mitch, we discussed anal tongue sex the other night. I know you're gay. In fact, I'm pretty sure the first time we met, you were wearing a rainbow tie-dyed T-shirt that said, 'I'm gay.' "

He barked a laugh and shook his head. "I wouldn't be caught dead in tie-dyed anything. It was just a rainbow."

"Whatever you say. Hey, before you get rollin' again...I was supposed to get your bacon. Just throw it on my plate."

Mitch glanced down at his salad and frowned. He scooped up a few bacon chunks with his fork and tossed them in the general direction of my plate. "Oops. They're a little slippery."

"Use your fingers. I don't care."

He obeyed with a laugh, then wiped his hands on a spare napkin and picked up his fork. "Happy now?"

"Ecstatic. Start talking. You want to make a YouTube video with me in it. Is that right?"

"Not exactly. I want to do an *Is It Real or Isn't It?* series featuring you and me...as a couple," he blurted.

"A couple of what?" I asked around a bite of hamburger.

Mitch held eye contact until he finished chewing; then he set his fork down and reached for his water. "This is the part where I need to ask you to listen and be open-minded. If you're not interested, I won't be offended but—"

"I'm listening."

"Okay. The premise is fairly simple. We would make a series of ten-to-fifteen-minute videos entitled 'Is This Real?' and post them intermittently over the course of the semester. The idea is to explore stereotyping and gather statistics about the perceived reality in social media. My following is small potatoes compared to some of the more popular YouTubers, but I have a decent base for this project. In the first video, we'll begin by announcing we're boyfriends."

"Boyfriends?" I repeated.

"Yes. At the end we'll make a 'Real or Not Real' statement, but it's all based on the premise that we're a couple. Viewers might not believe we are, but we'll ask them to play along and weigh in. For instance, episode one...we're a new couple. Real or not real? Episode two, we talk about things we've learned about each other. Evan loves bacon and french fries, and he gets a little cranky when he's hungry. Real or not real? Get it?"

I furrowed my brow and set my half-eaten hamburger aside. "I think so. You want us to be pretend boyfriends."

"Not really 'pretend.' We're not trying to fool our friends or family. It's only for the project. We want viewers to wonder and maybe question why they become invested in the lives and relationships of strangers."

"Do you really think anyone will care if we're 'real' or not?"

"You'd be surprised. I told you people follow YouTubers religiously. This is a good way to explore the 'actual' reality behind so-called reality TV. Audiences love couples. I'm gay and out and proud. Obviously I need a male partner. And you're perfect because you're my exact opposite and yet...we have things in common."

"Like what?"

"We're both athletes. I'm a gymnast, and you're a football player."

"You're a yell leader," I reminded him with a frown.

"I'm a trained gymnast." Mitch narrowed his eyes and huffed. He played with the condensation on the side of his glass before continuing, "I know this is weird. I'm only asking because you said you're open the other night. Your exact words were something like 'Love is love, sex is sex, and sexuality is fluid.' Ring any bells?"

"Yeah, but that doesn't mean I'm looking for a boyfriend."

"This is not real, Evan. *Ugh!* Why do straight men think every other gay guy wants to suck their cock?"

"Hang on. You don't want to suck my dick?" I asked in mock confusion.

He smirked. "Of course I do."

"You *really* do, or are you fucking with me?"

"I'm totally fucking with you," he replied with a straight face. Then he cocked his head and bit his bottom lip in a seductive gesture that made my mouth go dry. "Or am I?"

"Uh...I can't tell."

"See?" He slapped his hand on the table and grinned like a madman. "It's perfect! The hint of intrigue. Is this for real? Are Mitch and Evan actually a couple? And supposing they are, what's their relationship like? What do they really know about each other? It's like a mini version of the Newlywed Game. *Faux* or no?" He gasped and snapped his fingers. "That's what we'll call it! Damn, I'm a genius."

"Except our friends and family will know it's fake. Someone we know will weigh in online and ruin it. It won't work," I said.

"Yes, it will. It's called acting. I don't know about your family, but my grandmother has no idea what YouTube is, and she wouldn't watch if she did. As far as our friends are concerned... we won't actively lie, but they may start to wonder if we spend time together doing boyfriendy things."

"Like what, kissing?"

I was kidding and I fully expected Mitch to roll his eyes and tell me not to be ridiculous. But he tilted his head and gave me a thoughtful look that made me nervous. My pulse accelerated as I waited for him to continue.

"Maybe," he said, drawing out the two-syllable word until it seemed like a full sentence. "Have you ever kissed a guy?"

"No," I lied.

"Would you kiss me?"

I stared at his full lips for a moment and then met his eyes. "Uh…"

Mitch smiled. It was a slow, knowing grin with a flirtatious edge I should have found humorous because…he had to be joking, right? Or was this a seduction of some kind? And why couldn't I tell?

His nose twitched with delight before he snickered. "You're kind of adorkable. But don't worry. You're charming and very good-looking, but I'm not interested in converting you to my gay religion. You're safe with me, Evan."

"That's strangely disappointing," I quipped.

"It's not my style to throw myself at a straight man. Even a sexy one. When you eventually decide you can't live without me, you'll have to win me over the old-fashioned way. You know, draw our names in the sand in a heart at the beach. That kind of thing."

"Gotcha. All right. I'll do it."

"Do what? The heart in the sand? I'm open to other gestures too. Skywriting would be cool."

"And expensive," I snarked. "Don't get carried away. I meant, I'll be your project boyfriend."

"Really?" He dropped his fork on his plate and grinned.

"Sure. It sounds easy enough. We do a few videos, answer a few questions, and maybe kiss once in a while, right? If we throw in a couple of lunch dates like this one, people might think we're the real thing. I bet they think we're boyfriends now."

"I doubt it. Boyfriends are more touchy. You'd have to act like you want me. Like you're thinking about what we did in bed thirty minutes ago and the memory alone is giving you palpitations."

"Palpitations or a hard-on?"

Mitch shot a wicked grin at me as he speared a piece of spinach. "Yes."

"I can do that," I said confidently. "When do we start?"

"Immediately. And thank you. This is going to be a kickass project! I'm gonna owe you big time. More so if it gets me into grad school. What's your schedule like this week?"

"Practice, class, game on Saturday. Game days vary, but otherwise it's the same basic schedule through November. What about you?" I asked before popping the last of my burger in my mouth.

"Same. It sounds like neither of us has much free time. Are you sure you won't mind spending yours with me?" Mitch inclined his head. "The boyfriend thing may mess with your booty call game. If this isn't working for you at any time, let me know. Or if you see a potential hazard, like a girl you want to ask out or—"

"That won't happen."

"How can you be so sure?"

I smacked his hand when he reached into the basket of fries. "Because I'm super focused during season. This is my last and I'm making the most of it. No distractions. I'll go to a few social events because it's expected. But I won't stay long or party like a rock star. And as much as I like sex, I don't want to get involved with anyone who might mess with my game."

"Sex messes with your game?" he asked dubiously.

"No. It actually helps my game. It's the emotional BS I can't handle. I'm not a smooth operator. I tend to put my foot in my mouth, and then I feel bad about it and inevitably it fucks with my head. I'll be on the field, waiting for the whistle to blow, thinking about what I should have said or done instead of paying attention to the ball. Not okay."

"Hmm. Makes sense." He held his hand above the basket of fries and gave me another mischievous look. "So let's talk french fries. Boyfriends share and—"

"Nope."

"What do you mean 'nope'? I gave you my bacon. You upped my side of fries order to a trough, Evan. But it was always *my* order. You have to share. It's a perfect way to show your undying affection for me," he hummed.

"There are plenty of other ways to show fake affection," I assured him with a laugh.

"Not fake...faux. It sounds better," Mitch said, setting his napkin beside his plate before leaning in. "Show me what you got. Prove your faux affection for me."

"Now?" I took a quick glance around at the nearby tables. Everyone was engrossed in their own conversations. None of which were as weird as this one, I bet.

"Yep."

The challenge in his gaze was filled with humor. I had a feeling he didn't expect much from me on this project. He'd probably script easygoing dialogue and include a random kiss to throw people off once in a while. No doubt I was his third or fourth choice, filling in for someone else...like Rory. In fact, I was suddenly sure of it, and the idea pissed me off for no good reason at all. My niggling sense of misplaced jealousy made me want to surprise the hell out of him.

"Okay, fine." I wiped my mouth, then stood abruptly and moved to his side.

Mitch looked up at me and frowned. "Are you leaving?"

"No."

"Then wha—"

I cupped his face in my hands and pressed my lips against his.

The kiss was meant to shut him up and throw him off stride. And okay, maybe I hoped he'd forget his name for half a second and realize I should have always been his first choice. A harmless kiss to seal the deal seemed like a good way to counteract negativity and prove I was fully onboard.

But I hadn't counted on his lips being so damn soft. I sank

into the connection and lost myself for a moment. He was sweet and seductive and fuck, he felt amazing. I wanted to taste him and smell him. I rubbed my thumbs over his jaw and sucked on his lower lip to keep myself from pushing my tongue inside his mouth. The desire was real but my timing was off.

I backed up slowly and moved to my chair with a lopsided smile that I hoped exuded confidence I didn't feel. It could have been a total fail. Mitch's shocked expression didn't bode well. I had to say something. Anything.

"How was that?" I winced. *Lame.*

"*What* was that?" he asked, touching two fingers to his bottom lip.

"A boyfriend kiss. The spontaneous in-public kind that should convince the average passerby that I'm into you. How'd I do?"

Mitch nodded slowly and absently reached for his water. "Very, very well. You're hired," he deadpanned.

I busted up laughing and held my hand out for a high five. "Gee, thanks."

"I appreciate this, Evan. I know I'm asking a lot. More than the average friend of a friend should. If you want to get back to me tomorrow or—"

"Let's not overthink this. It's an assignment or a friend helping a friend." I pulled my wallet out of my pocket and set my credit card over the leather folder the waiter left between us. "The way I see it, life is short. I don't want to be cautious or careful, and I don't want to say no to any challenge that comes along. When I die, I want to know I lived. That's all."

Mitch nodded slowly. "Okay. Well, next step...we need to go over a schedule. We'll have to rehearse before we film for the first time. We need to check lighting, angles, and go over material. And we'll have to plan a few appearances. Nothing major. A trip to a coffee shop will work. Be prepared for selfie central. If your selfie game is weak, I can give you pointers. I'll create a joint account for us on other platforms, like Instagram. Do you have Instagram?"

I shook my head and chuckled at his flabbergasted expression. "I don't have time. I barely check Facebook."

"Oh, boy. I'll handle it. And not to worry, I won't post anything without your approval."

"I trust you, Mitch."

"Thanks. For everything. I think we're about to do something amazing. I can't wait," he gushed.

We shared a smile that felt like a handshake or signing our names on a dotted line side-by-side. Or some version of a commitment that came with a virtual eraser. This wasn't binding. It was just for fun. A new way to push old boundaries and to remind myself that complacency was a form of death. And I wasn't giving in or giving up yet.

3

W e agreed to meet the following evening at his place to begin what Mitch referred to as "basic boyfriend lessons." According to him, we needed at least a one-hour rehearsal before we attempted to do anything in front of a camera. We lived a few blocks away from each other, which made an end-of-day meeting convenient. I showered at school after my second practice and grabbed something to eat on campus to avoid traffic and ended up arriving fifteen minutes early. I thought about going home, but it hardly seemed worth the trip. Besides, I didn't want to chance running into Derek. Not until I had my story down.

I parked my battered Highlander on the street in front of a pristine white stucco house with green shutters and pretty window boxes. A low hedge lined the path to the front door decorated with a giant floral wreath. I didn't see the garage, though. I pulled out my cell and reread Mitch's last text message as I stepped onto the front porch.

Park in the alley behind the street. I'll be home by 8. Come any time after.

I glanced at the time. Seven forty-five. *Hmm.* I could wait in my truck or—

"Hello, dear. Can I help you?"

I jumped back in surprise and almost landed flat on my ass. "Oh! Yeah, um…I'm sorry. I'm—I'm looking for Mitch."

An old woman wearing a leopard print tracksuit stood in the open doorway. She had snow-white hair and sinewy, birdlike features that gave her a fragile look. But the mischievous glint in her blue-shadowed eyes hinted at a sense of humor that reminded me of Mitch. She must be his grandmother.

"Mitchell should be home soon. He usually pops inside to say hello, but I haven't seen him yet. Stay where you are for a sec. The boy's got big opinions about safety. Let me give him a call real quick. What did you say your name was?"

"Evan. Evan di Angelo," I said, offering her my hand.

"Aren't you charming?" She smiled brightly and shook my hand. Then she pulled a huge phone from her pocket and pushed a button before holding it to her ear. "Hello, sweetheart. You have a visitor. A handsome young man named Ivan."

"Evan." I corrected her in a low voice.

"Oh. It's Evan. Evan of the angels. That's what your name means, dear." She patted my hand, then refocused on her conversation with a series of "mmmhmms" before addressing me again. "Mitchell would like to speak with you. He sounds flustered. That must mean he likes you."

I stared at the bedazzled hot pink case for a second before taking the cell and putting it to my ear. "Hi, Mitchell."

"You're early and you're in the wrong place. You were supposed to meet me in the alley, not at my grandmother's front door."

"I'm good. How are you?" I replied flippantly.

I tried not to chuckle when he growled in response. I could just imagine him stuck at a traffic light on Pacific Coast Highway with steam coming from his ears. In a way, I understood. My parents were excruciatingly embarrassing whenever I brought friends over. I always worried they'd dig out my baby books. It had happened before, so it wasn't entirely outside the realm of possibility.

"Ugh. I'll be there in five minutes or less."

"Take your time...honey." I disconnected the call, then handed his grandmother her phone. "Thanks. He'll be here soon. I can wait in my truck."

"Nonsense! Come inside," she insisted.

She held the door open, pausing in the foyer to give me a thorough once-over. "Are you hungry? I made raspberry thumbprint cookies today. Mitchell's favorite. You can test them out for me and tell me all about yourself while you wait. I'm Maryanne, by the way."

"It's nice to meet you." I returned her megawatt grin and followed her through what could only be described as a time warp.

Plastic runners protected gold carpet in the formal living room. The furniture had an old but well-preserved look as though it had rarely been used. Family photographs covered the walls. She moved slowly enough that I was able to tell most of the pictures were of a younger Maryanne with two boys, whom I assumed were her sons. Once we moved into the adjoining family room, the decor changed to something a bit more modern. A comfy looking sectional and recliner were positioned in front of a large flat-screen television opposite the open family-style kitchen.

And every inch of wall space here was dedicated to Mitch. Baby, toddler, grade school, high school, and college. I moved closer to examine a particularly cute studio pic of a towheaded, blue-eyed Mitch holding a raggedy-looking stuffed rabbit by the ears. Maryanne stepped beside me and pointed at the glass.

"My Mitchell was four years old here. I've never seen a more beautiful child in my life. And I'm not just saying that because he's my grandson. Look at that face. Gorgeous, isn't he?" She turned to me with a radiant grin and winked. "Let's get you that cookie."

She pointed at a round dining table situated between the living and kitchen areas and instructed me to sit while she rustled up a few goodies. She reappeared a minute later with a plate and a stack of napkins.

"Thanks," I said as I reached for a cookie.

"Enjoy. I put water in the kettle for tea for you boys too. Green tea. No caffeine to mess with your slumber. Unless you want that. You can choose. I have plain ol' Lipton's too. Or coffee. Would you prefer coffee?"

"No, thank you. Wow. These are delicious."

"This is an old family recipe. My grandmother made these for me many moons ago," she replied with a laugh. "She lived three blocks away from this very house—if you can believe that."

"Oh. That's cool. So you're from Long Beach originally?" I asked politely.

"Yes. I've lived here almost all of my life. I raised my own family in this house. It didn't always look like this. The kitchen wasn't as fancy, and a few rooms were added here and there. But I've been here for forty-odd years. Let me tell you...time flies!" she chuckled.

I smiled and nodded in agreement. "Is Mitch your only grandson?"

"Yes." Her eyes took on a faraway look as though she was bracing herself against something painful. "I had two sons. Calvin died far too young, and the other is Wyatt, Mitchell's father. I don't see him often. He's a busy man. An important chef in Hollywood. Mitchell looked a bit like his dad when he was a child, but now I think he resembles his mother's side of the family. She's a cracker for sure."

"A cracker?"

"Oh, yes." Maryanne rolled her eyes and huffed. "I suppose we're all some kind of a cracker, aren't we? Some people are Ritz crackers or plain ol' Saltines, and others like to think of themselves as one of those artisan brands that you can only buy in specialty stores."

I grinned. "And what are you?"

She leaned forward and patted my hand. "I'm not a cracker at all. I'm a cookie. A raspberry thumbprint cookie, I reckon. Depending on the weather and how they're stored, these cookies can be soft or hard on the outside, but they're always sweet in the center. Mitchell is the same way. Don't let that boy fool you, dear. He's the kindest soul you'll ever meet and very sensitive. When Mitchell was three years old he—"

"Oh. My. God." Mitch entered through the kitchen and cast a wide-eyed look between us before zeroing in on his grandmother. "You fed him cookies?"

"Well, of course. We're just getting to know each other. I like your new boyfriend. He's a nice young man—and so handsome too," she gushed, patting my hand affectionately before gazing up at Mitch. "How was your day, dear?"

"I—it was fine. But it just got weird," he groused. "Grams, Evan and I are gonna head upstairs now."

"All right, then take your tea with you. And the cookies," she insisted.

She was up and out of her seat before either of us could argue. Mitch flopped into the chair she vacated and gave me a lopsided smile. "This is what happens when you're early."

"I don't mind. I like her. She fed me cookies *and* told me I'm handsome," I said.

Mitch's smile grew. "She's pretty awesome. But she talks a lot. I hoped to avoid a prolonged family history lesson. Nothing scares guys away faster than your grandmother whipping out your naked baby photos one minute and pledging her support for gay marriage the next. Whatever. You aren't likely to fall in love with me, so I guess it doesn't matter. But if you don't mind, it's easier if she thinks we really are boyfriends. She's a serious romantic and it would take a lot of time to explain why—"

"Here you go! I've assembled a few snacks for you boys." Maryanne sailed into the room, carrying a tray overladen with a teapot, cups, and cookies.

I stood to grab the tray before she tipped it against the table. Mitch hiked his bag on his shoulder and hugged his grandmother. "Thanks, Grams. Did you take your medicine?"

She knit her brow thoughtfully and pulled a small box from her pocket. "What day is it?"

"Tuesday. If the box is empty, you're okay. Remember, we're just doing one day at a time now," Mitch said gently.

She shook the box and then opened it.

"Empty. Now go on and have fun. It was nice to meet you, dear. We have so much more to talk about," she said to me before stepping backward. "Such a handsome couple. You look like salt and pepper shakers. One light, one dark, but you sure go together nicely."

"Right. Good night, Grams." Mitch kissed her cheek and waited for me to say good-bye before ushering me through the kitchen, out the side door, and into a courtyard.

A giant oak tree dominated the space. We walked around the perimeter to a set of stairs next to an unattached garage. I adjusted the tray in my arms before following him to his studio. Mitch hurried ahead to unlock the door. He held it open and then gestured for me to set the tray on the mini standalone island next to the kitchenette. I obeyed, glancing at my surroundings while Mitch poured tea for us.

The apartment was the size of a semi-generous hotel room with a queen-sized bed on one end under a window and a kitchenette on the opposite side. I couldn't see the bathroom, but it was probably located where the wall cut off next to the sink. The decor was mid-century modern or a perfect blend of his grandmother's formal living and family rooms...minus the personal photos. The walls were white and the funky art over his bed complemented the primary color palette of the duvet.

"Nice place," I commented as I perched on one of the barstools at the tiny island.

"I like it. It's close to school, the beach, and...family. Sometimes a little *too* close to family but that's okay. She needs me now. I don't mind. I'm giving you green tea, by the way. Lipton sucks." Mitch pushed a white teacup toward me, then skirted the island and sat down. "Help yourself to another cookie too."

"Thanks. She's cool. You're lucky to still have grandparents around. I only have one. My grandmother lives in Italy. We used to visit once a year when we were kids, but it got expensive for a family of four to travel. I haven't been since the acci—it's been a few years," I finished quickly before stuffing a cookie in my mouth.

"So you're Italian?"

"Half Italian, half Irish." I brushed my hands on my jeans and narrowed my gaze. "Is she okay? You seemed kinda worried about her."

Mitch shot a surprised glance at me. "She had a heart attack last year. She's fine now, but she fell a few months ago and suddenly, she's forgetting things she shouldn't. Like taking her medicine. I've started separating her pills daily instead of weekly, but it doesn't always help. She's pretty spry for eighty-three and sharp too, but the doctor said it wasn't unusual for mild dementia to be a side effect of a fall at her age. So yeah...I worry about her." He waited a beat and added, "And I *really* worry when I think about what she said to you in the ten measly minutes you were alone with her. Grams has no filter. That's not new, though. She's always been that way."

"She didn't say much. She talked about your parents and—"

"What?" he asked, widening his eyes comically.

"Don't freak out. She didn't tell any big secrets."

Mitch sighed wearily. "We don't see my parents often. They

divorced about ten years ago. Mom went to New York to see if she could make it on Broadway. I see her once a year. Maybe. And Dad is a so-called celebrity chef. If I'm lucky, I see him less than that. It's just Grams and me. She's been taking care of me for a while now, so it's my turn to take care of her. What about you? I should probably know where you're from and how many siblings you have for this project."

"I'm from Pasadena. I have one younger brother, Eli. He's a junior at Pepperdine. My dad teaches biology at the city college and my mom is an astrophysicist. She works at JPL."

He cocked his head curiously. "What does that stand for again?"

"NASA Jet Propulsion Lab."

"Whoa. You've got some smart folks in your family," he drawled in a hick accent.

"And then there's me. I didn't get any of their science or math smarts. I took my time in college so I could play football, but I have no idea what comes next."

"I don't either. Grad school, I hope. But the future is a mystery. You have to take it one day at a time and work hard to make good things happen."

I stared at him in awe for a moment. It was like he read my mind and was reciting my daily mantra back to me. Although some days, mine had a more desperate edge to it. *You've got this. Don't fuck it up.*

"Positive thinking helps," I replied lamely as I lifted my cup to my mouth. I sipped the green tea and winced. *Yuck.* No wonder I never drank tea.

Mitch snickered. "Do you want water or coffee instead? I have ginger kombucha too. But since it's basically fermented tea, you won't like that either. And that stuff is expensive. I'm not sharing if you don't love it."

"Keep the tea. I'll take you up on that water, though. Please," I added.

"You got it." He stood gracefully and moved to the other side of the mini island. He grabbed a water bottle from an open shelf and slid it toward me. "This is actually a very helpful exercise. It ties in neatly with what I wanted to go over tonight. Likes and dislikes. I figured we could play a quick game of Either Or, take a few selfies and...I think we need a signature move."

"Signature move? I don't like the sound of that."

"It'll be fun," he insisted.

"Keep talking." I uncapped the water bottle and took a healthy swig.

"Okay. Here's what I'm thinking." Mitch tapped his fingers rhythmically, then paced the two feet to the sink and back again. "An icebreaker game is perfect for an opening episode. We get to know each other a little more, and our audience gets to know us. We'll keep it simple. Chocolate or vanilla?"

I frowned. "That's not even a question. Chocolate."

"Cat or dog, Netflix and chill or party, beach or pool, tropics or mountains?"

"Dog, Netflix, beach and...hmm, both," I replied quickly.

"Look at us! Already we're so compatible! But I say tropics over mountains. I'm dying to go back to Hawaii. Anyway, you get the idea. I have more interesting questions, and obviously we can ad-lib too."

"Sounds easy. And the signature move?"

Mitch put his hands over his mouth as though holding back a bubble of laughter. "Yes, a dance."

"I don't dance," I deadpanned.

"Of course you do! Football players are great dancers. You'll be awesome."

"No, thanks. I'm awesome enough as is."

"This move will make you triple-awesome," Mitch assured me with a Cheshire cat grin. "Check it out."

He stepped backward and swung his arms over his head.

Then he brought them down low and shook his ass. He repeated the sequence and ended with an "air" high five.

"I'm not doin' that."

"Try it. Just once. Pretty please," he singsonged.

I held his sugary stare with an unfriendly one that should have made him drop the subject instantly. When he didn't look away, I sighed dramatically and stood. "Fine. Once. That's it."

Mitch whooped and hurried to join me on the other side of the island. "Super easy. Hands in the air like this. Oh, wait. We need music."

"No, we don't."

Mitch ignored me. He pulled his cell from his pocket, pushed a few keys, and set it on the counter before standing in front of me. "Okay. Hands in the air, then bring 'em down, back up again, shake your booty, high five."

I followed his instructions with a scowl firmly in place. I was about to lift my arms a second time when Miley Cyrus's "Party in the USA" blasted through his home speaker system.

"Are you kidding me with this song?"

Mitch danced around me, bopping to the beat and humming along. "This song is perfect! It's happy and fun, and it makes you want to dance. We can't play it on the video for copyright reasons, but it's a good song to have in your head when you're shakin' your ass. Come on, Ev. Don't give me the monster mash version. Shake it like you mean it!"

He did his "hands up, down, shake it" dance, adding a sexy grind and snap and signaled for me to join in. I played along for the duration of the song for a couple of reasons. One, it seemed kind of dickish not to participate and two, his silly sense of fun was contagious.

When the song finally ended, I gave him a bro-style shoulder nudge and laughed. "Don't tell me we're doing that for three minutes."

"God, no! We'd lose our audience within fifteen seconds. The itinerary is short and simple. Intro, content, closing song, done. The intro will go something like this..." Mitch cleared his throat and stared into the distance, then said, "Count me in."

"Uh...one, two—"

"No, no. Always count backward in show biz and in this instance, start at five." He waited for me to comply. When I reached "one," his smile grew and lit his handsome face. "Hi, I'm Mitch and this is my boyfriend, Evan. Or is he? We're starting a new game on my channel called 'Faux or No?' Make sure you hit the 'subscribe' button so you can weigh in. Over the next couple of months, we're going to give you a teensy glimpse into our relationship. Nothing too kinky. We won't be filming in bed...unless Evan says so."

I frowned when he pointed at me with an expectant look. "What do you want me to say?"

Mitch rolled his eyes. "If I told you we were filming in bed, how would you respond?"

"Fuck, no."

"Exactly. Except...no swearing. Let's try it again."

"But that's what I'd say. Why censor it?"

"Because I love the F-word as much as anyone else, but it doesn't translate well on these kinds of videos. It's not a problem to say it once in a while, but it can't be everyone's first impression of you."

"Why the fuck not?" I challenged.

Mitch scoffed. "Now you're just being a real fuckhead. Cooperate, please. This is your intro. Oh, and maybe you should put your arm around me and kiss my cheek."

"Now?"

"Yes. This is a rehearsal, so...go for it."

I moved to his side, slipped my arm around his waist, and kissed his cheek. His scruff threw me off stride. It wasn't noticeable because his facial hair was blond, but I could feel it. He smelled and felt different from anyone I'd ever kissed before.

Sure, I'd kissed male relatives. I was part Italian. No one in my family shied from physical contact. But a hug and kiss on each cheek from my Uncle Gianni was different from kissing an attractive man. I caressed his cheek impulsively and then leaned in to sniff him the way I'd wanted to since the party. "Mmm."

"What are you doing?" he asked.

"You smell good. I've never kissed a guy I wasn't related to who had a five o'clock shadow."

Mitch gave me a funny look. "You kissed me yesterday at lunch."

"Yeah, but you haven't shaved since this morning, right? The texture is like sandpaper...but in a good way. I like it," I assured him.

He looked flustered for a second but recovered quickly. "Well, that'll make the real kiss easier then."

"Right. When do we kiss, and what's the intensity level supposed to be? G, PG, PG-13? Or are we going straight to the nasty?" I teased.

"Ha. G is peck on the cheek, which we just covered. PG is peck on the lips. That should be fine."

"Got it. Maybe we should practice first," I said.

"Um...sure." Mitch turned around and gestured toward the bar stools at the island. "We can sit there, and I'll set up the tripod a foot or so from where you're standing now."

"We don't have to be in exact position. I just need to get used to touching you. It would be the same with anyone. Guy or girl."

Okay, fine. I wanted to do it again. I'd thought about him nonstop since the party last weekend. And that throwaway kiss yesterday at the restaurant had opened a Pandora's box. I was consumed now. I didn't *want* to practice kissing him. I *had* to or I'd go crazy.

"Maybe you're right. Um...okay. You can kiss me," he said in a low voice.

"Well, you have to participate," I chided as I stepped into his space.

"I'm...yes. Do you want to go first? Like..." Mitch set his hand on my hip and inched closer still. "...this?"

I lifted my right hand and hovered it above his ear for a moment before threading my fingers through his hair. He suddenly looked nervous, which somehow worked in my favor. I held his gaze, then moved forward and gently pressed my lips to his. And fuck, it felt amazing to be here again. I tilted my head slightly, loving the intoxicating contrast of his soft lips and scratchy chin. Mitch closed his eyes and hooked his arms around my neck so we stood toe-to-toe and chest-to-chest. All the ways this felt different no longer applied. I knew what to do here. I was practically a fucking expert.

I cradled the back of his neck and licked his bottom lip. He let me in immediately, gliding his tongue alongside mine in a slow, sexy maneuver that made my pulse race. My instincts screamed for me to keep going. I owed it to myself to see where this led. I deepened the connection, twisting my tongue with his in a building frenzy. Then I lowered my hand down his back and pulled him against me, so my half-hard cock grazed his—

Oh, fuck.

I released him quickly and swiped my hand across my mouth as I tried to think of how to defuse any potential awkwardness. The best method for dealing with uncertainty was humor, but nothing seemed particularly funny at the moment. My heart was pounding, my brain felt fuzzy, and the longer I stared at his swollen lips, the more I wanted to pull him close again and see what might happen next.

Mitch looked like he felt the same. A little shell-shocked but definitely curious. I started forward but just as my momentum shifted, I lost my nerve.

I gulped and let out a strained half chuckle. "Was that what you had in mind?"

"Uh...y-yeah. Um, let's just go through a few questions." He bit his bottom lip and fuck, that was hotter than it should have been. "I flagged fifty good ones that—"

"Fifty?" I asked incredulously.

"Well, yeah. There are a lot of categories. Food, music and...sex."

"Oookay."

"I know...weird. But sex sells and if we really were a couple, we'd be thinking about it constantly. Didn't you say it's practically part of our DNA at the party?"

"True. I'm thinking about it right now," I said unthinkingly.

"You are?"

"Yeah, but..."

"But what?" he prodded.

"That kiss..." I paced to the door and back. "That was fucking hot. If you ask me one sex question, I might actually come in my jeans."

"Are you sure you aren't bi?" he asked, furrowing his brow.

"I never said I wasn't," I countered.

"Right. You said 'fluid,' which probably means 'curious.' Okay, I can work with that," he said with a naughty lopsided grin before picking up his cell and perching on one of the barstools. "Let's continue, shall we?"

"Bring it on."

I flopped onto the stool next to him and studied his profile as he scrolled through his phone, aware that I was sitting closer than necessary. My leg was less than an inch from his. But that would be normal if we really were a couple. In fact, we'd be in constant contact. Lovers touched unconsciously. Didn't they? Of course, I was no expert. I hadn't been in a relationship that lasted longer than three months in a while.

My theory was worth testing, though. I rested my knee against his and waited with my heart in my throat to see what he'd do.

Nothing. *Hmm.* Interesting.

"*Pretty Little Liars* or *Real Housewives*?"

My gaze shifted from our knees to his mouth and all I could think was, *Damn, I want to kiss him again. And touch him and*—I refocused when I caught his expectant look. I ran the question he'd asked through my head and scowled.

"No stupid questions allowed."

Mitch snorted. "It's not stupid. It's—"

"Just move on to the sex."

"Are you sure?" He snickered when I rolled my eyes; then he sat up tall on his barstool and crossed his legs so we were no longer touching. I didn't like the loss of contact, but it was probably for the best. My awareness of him was freaking me out.

"Positive."

"Would you rather have sex in a public bathroom or library?"

"Bathroom," I replied immediately.

Mitch squinted at me. "Have you ever?"

"Yeah, have you?"

He pursed his lips and nodded. "Yes. Um, next question. Lights on or off? Missionary or doggie? Sex toys or—"

"Hold on. You're moving kinda fast there, cowboy. Let's see…if I can only choose one, lights on, missionary, and yes to sex toys. You?"

"Missionary?"

"Yeah, I'm a visual person. You can't tell if your partner is having as much fun as you are unless you can see for yourself," I said.

"You can see if your positions are reversed too."

"Obviously."

"No, I meant like…if your partner is riding you, ya know?"

I gave him a sly sideways grin and nodded. "Yeah, I know what you mean. Giddy up, cowboy. I prefer being on top. Maybe that's something you should know."

Mitch snorted in amusement. "Right. Thanks for sharing. I

guess what I'm trying to say is that if you're with the right person, you can tell without seeing their expression."

"What does that have to do with your favorite position?"

"I don't know," he said, sounding flustered. "Let's move on. Do you—"

"Wait. I have another question. By 'right person,' do you mean a soul mate? Have you ever had that?"

Mitch cocked his head and then shook it. "No. Have you?"

"No. Not even close." I paused for a moment before continuing. "What about Rory?"

"No. I liked him a lot, but we didn't connect on a deep level. Too much fear in the way. People at school probably guessed he was bi, but he wasn't ready to be truly out. I wouldn't have even asked him to do this show with me. He would have felt too exposed. Rory couldn't handle the possibility of anyone thinking he might be attracted to a guy. When I realized he was always going to fixate on how others saw him and how it made him feel, I knew we were over. It's too bad. The sex was amazing."

His saucy smile went well with his flippant delivery, but I was too unsettled to appreciate it and I couldn't say why. Okay, that was a lie. I was jealous again. Very, very jealous. An ugly green haze clouded my vision and made it difficult to see straight. And why? Because I didn't like that he had sex with his boyfriend? That didn't make sense. Nonetheless, the thought of him riding Rory cowboy-style made my blood boil.

"Hmph. Well, Rory's an idiot." I stood abruptly and hooked my thumb toward the door. "I'm gonna go. When do you want to film this?"

"Next week is good," he said with a frown. He joined me at the door but tugged at my belt loop before I could open it. "Hey, are you mad or something?"

"Why would I be?"

"I don't know. *You* brought up Rory, not me."

I winced. "I know. I just—the Rory thing is...weird. I don't like the guy."

"It's over, so don't worry about it."

"Yeah." I nodded and put my hand on the doorknob. Then I turned to face him and shook my head wildly. "That's not really it. I—that kiss was intense. Or was that just me?"

"It was very intense." Mitch went still and licked his lips. "PG-13 for sure. It doesn't have to be like that on the post. We can tone it down a bit or even take it out altogether."

"No. I liked it. I'm..." I let out a rush of air and then shrugged awkwardly. "I'm gonna tell you a secret. No one knows this. And I mean no one. Not even Derek."

"You can trust me."

I studied him for a moment thoughtfully. "I lied about kissing a guy."

"Okay..."

I inclined my head and rambled on in what had to sound like the world's longest run-on sentence. "When I was thirteen, I was at a party and a group of kids decided to play Spin the Bottle. I didn't know how it worked, so like a true dumbshit, I volunteered to go first. I spun the bottle and said a silent prayer it landed on Emily Korbel. I had a mini crush on her. We kissed once at the homecoming dance in a dark corner of the gym. One of those lip to lip things. No big deal. I was hoping for another shot but instead...it landed on Brian Markus. Everyone went crazy. They hollered for us to 'kiss, kiss, kiss' and I didn't know what to do. I froze. But Brian seemed okay with it. He whispered something to me like, "Do it fast and get it over with." So I did and...it wasn't so bad at all. I actually kind of liked it. His lips were soft, and he smelled like peppermint. I thought about it nonstop for years. That kiss fueled a few memorable jack-off sessions. I always wanted to tell him that but I didn't dare. Do you understand?"

I went quiet and willed Mitch to intervene and tell me he got what I was trying to say. Of course, I didn't really understand myself, but…that didn't have to mean anything.

"Evan, you were in junior high," he said patiently. "No one's going to hold a Spin the Bottle gay kiss against you. It doesn't mean you're more like me either, so if that's your big secret, don't let it keep you up at night."

"That's not it at all," I huffed and pushed my fingers through my hair in frustration. "Look, I-I've done it more than once with another guy too."

"You did?" he asked, clearly confused.

"But…it never felt like this. I liked kissing you. I liked it yesterday at lunch, and I liked doing it a few minutes ago even more. Your lips are soft and sweet, and you smell better than peppermint. That's all."

Mitch opened his mouth and closed it twice. "Thank you."

"Next week, same day?" I asked, turning the doorknob.

"Um, Tuesday won't work. Let's say Thursday. I have to cheer at the men's volleyball game that night, but I should be home by eight. Fair warning, if you get here early, you risk having tea and cookies with my grandmother again."

"I don't mind."

Mitch's smile morphed into a radiant grin that poured from him like sunshine. I stared for a moment, admiring his golden hair and pretty eyes. *Fuck.* No, that adjective wasn't strong enough. His eyes were beautiful. Hell, *he* was beautiful and…

And I was seconds away from creeping myself out. What was wrong with me?

"You're a good guy, Ev. I'll see you next time. You can get to your car through the side gate. It'll lead you to the street. Park in the alley behind the garage next time. Oh…and wear black," he said as I stepped onto the landing.

"Why black?"

"So we can coordinate," he replied matter-of-factly.

"No way. If we were a real couple, I'd go out of my way not to match with you," I huffed.

Mitch chuckled. "Not matching. Coordinating. It's a lighting and general aesthetic thing. We want to look visually pleasing on film. I can always change when you get here, but it's already going to be late and I don't want to waste any time."

"Hmph. I'll probably forget."

"I'll remind you."

"How long can it possibly take to film a ten-to-fifteen-minute segment?"

"A couple of hours."

"What? How?" I asked incredulously.

"There's a lot to it! Okay, maybe it won't take that much time. I'm not sure. I'll try to set up the lighting ahead of time, and we can rehearse a little so we're both comfortable. But once I press record, it's pretty free-flowing, which means we'll make mistakes, and I'll have to do a lot of editing. In this case, more is better. I don't want to be left with five minutes of nothing exciting."

"All right. Whatever you say."

"God, you're already a dream boyfriend," he commented in a swoony tone, batting his eyelashes. "Are you going to kiss me goodnight too?"

I barked a quick laugh and started down the steps. But halfway to the bottom, I turned back and met him at the door. Mitch cocked his head curiously, but he didn't flinch when I held his chin and kissed him. It was supposed to be lighthearted. Almost a joke. But when I pulled back, we stared at each other and smiled and...I had to do it again. The right way. I leaned in and hovered my lips over his and then licked the seam. He let me immediately. He hummed appreciatively, wrapping his arms around my neck and raking his fingers through my hair. I glided my tongue alongside his in a sweet, slow exploration that made me weak in the knees. I didn't pull back until we were breathless and in danger of heading someplace we couldn't easily navigate back from. I pulled away and then stepped aside.

"See ya," I said huskily before heading down the stairs and out the gate.

I hurried to my SUV, jumped inside, turned on the engine, and sped down the block. I came to a screeching halt at the stop sign at the end of the residential street. Adrenaline coursed through my veins. I felt oddly energized yet freaked out at the same time.

I knew why. I'd been here before, and I told myself I'd never do this again. And I'd been doing just fine until Mitch came along. I loosened my hold on the wheel and ran my finger over my bottom lip.

Fuck, I wanted him.

I wasn't mildly curious. I was consumed. I burned with a feverish intensity I'd never felt off a football field. Everything in me wanted to turn around now and tell him the truth. Explain who I was, what I wanted, and why I was so fucking afraid. Selling myself as a good guy who was willing to help a friend of a friend was dishonest. But the truth...that shit was scary. I'd been through hell and back five years ago because of my so-called truth. I had physical and mental scars, broken dreams, and a host of issues I never talked about anymore.

And if I did this project with Mitch and jumped into cyberland, pretending to be his boyfriend, I'd reveal myself. My friends, family, and teammates might not believe the boyfriend story, but they'd wonder what I was thinking. Eventually, the truth would come out. Was I ready for this?

I glanced into my rearview mirror when a car pulled up behind me. I nodded to myself and then shook my head ruefully. *Fuck, no.* But I wasn't backing down or bowing out. Not this time.

4

There was something surreal about launching into a mystery adventure I couldn't share with anyone. School and football kept me pretty busy over the next week, but I found myself thinking about Mitch constantly. Not the questions he'd ask or how this might play out over the next month or so. I thought about *him*. The way he walked and talked and the way his eyes sparked mischievously when he smiled. And yeah, I thought about kissing him. A lot.

When my head wouldn't stop spinning, I gave in and called him. At first, he gave me a hard time for not texting instead, but when I made up a story about my fingers cramping and possibly messing with my masturbation game, he laughed heartily. We talked every night after our respective classes, practices, or games. Sometimes he ran through some of his questions. It was a good way to ease into conversation.

"Coffee or tea?"

"Coffee."

"How do you take your coffee? It's not one of the official questions, but it's something a boyfriend would know," he explained.

"Black. How about you?"

"Same. Okay. Next...eggs or oatmeal? Donuts or cake? Corn or peas?"

"Eggs, both and corn. Peas are disgusting."

"You can't have both cake and donuts," Mitch huffed. "You have to choose."

"But it's true. If I had a slice of chocolate cake and a glazed donut in front of me, I'd put 'em both on my plate."

"And which would you eat first?"

"Whichever was closer." I grinned when he laughed aloud. Then I asked, "What about you?"

"Oatmeal, cake, and corn. Peas are nasty."

"The worst. My mom had a veggie rule when I was a kid. No dessert until all the vegetables on our plates were gone. I tried everything, man. I fed green beans to the dog, hid carrots under the throw rug when she wasn't looking. I even stuffed brussels sprouts in my pockets once. Nothing gets by my mom, though. The dog barfed up the beans, Dad stepped on the carrots, and let's just say she wasn't too happy about the mushy sprouts in her laundry."

Mitch chuckled. "I bet."

"But peas. Ugh. I sat forever waiting to be rescued from a plate of peas a few times—for a cookie. Torture."

"Poor Evan. Too bad you didn't know me back then. Grams would have hooked you up. She had a pretty relaxed view on veggie intake. I was a weird kid, though. I ate whatever she put in front of me without argument. I'd do anything to avoid going home," he said.

"Why? What was wrong with your folks?"

"They hated each other. They fought constantly. It was horrible. My strategy was to be as silent as possible, so they'd forget about me instead of using me as a weapon. I was a very quiet kid."

"You seem to have come out of your shell. I've seen you dancing on tables with Chelsea," I teased.

"That's different—she's my best friend. But you're right...it took awhile, but I eventually found my voice. I have my grandmother to thank for that. She's pretty open and outgoing. She didn't mind that I was quiet, but she didn't like the reasons. I moved in with her when I was thirteen and other than a short stint in the dorms, I haven't left. It's not because we're family," he said conversationally. "We're a team. Can't leave your teammates."

"Hmm. You're right."

I'd switched topics before I was tempted to share more than either of us bargained for. Mitch went with the flow. He had a good sense of humor and an easygoing vibe I appreciated. I liked our conversations. They felt honest and real.

When we'd hung up last night, he'd hinted at a few surprise questions he'd come up with for our Thursday meeting. I thought about coming up with a few of my own as I made my way out of the locker room the Wednesday beforehand. I pulled my cell out, intending to forward a funny blog post about new couples quirks to Mitch just as my phone buzzed in my hand.

"Hi, Mom. I'm about to walk into my Home Ec class. Want me to call you back later?"

My mother guffawed heartily. "Home Ec, eh? I don't want to keep you from learning how to boil water, dear. I just called to see how you are. How's the knee holding up?"

"Good. I'm supposed to see the sports therapist tomorrow."

"Will you be okay to play this Saturday?"

It was tempting to blow off her concern, but I'd given my parents cause to worry. Not recently, but some memories didn't fade quickly. I pushed away the instant and unwelcome *déjà vu* before replying.

"Yes. I'm fine. Will you and Dad be there?"

"Of course."

"Cool. I'll see you after the game." I moved up the stairs to my building but paused at the door when she didn't reply. "Mom?"

"Evan, Graham's dad passed away last week. His sister told me they'll plan a memorial service in a month or so, but his mom is —well, she's not doing well. Losing her son and now her husband...poor woman is heartbroken."

I swallowed hard and fixated on a bronze statue across the quad.

"What do you want me to do?" I whispered.

"Honey, you don't have to do anything. If you feel like sending a card, do it. If not, that's okay too. He was a good man and he tried so hard to...be there for you, even though he was hurting. I just wanted you to know. That's all. Are you okay?"

I blinked and nodded, though the gesture was lost on her. "Y-yeah."

An strained silence fell between us.

"Sweetheart, I'm sorry. I didn't mean to upset you."

"I'm not upset. I'm fine," I insisted weakly as I made my way back down the stairs. I sat on the corner of a stone bench and covered my face with my free hand.

"Go do something that makes you happy. Right now. Just...go buy a bag of M&Ms or splurge on one of those horrible slushies you like or call someone who makes you smile. Please?"

"Yeah. I will and I'm...okay."

"I love you, Ev," she said fervently. "To the next galaxy and back. No matter what."

I let out a half laugh and bit the inside of my cheek. "I love you too."

I disconnected the call and took a deep breath. And then another. The sky was blue, the sun shining, but I could practically see the darkness coming for me. Any second now, the sickening twist of metal would ring in my ear. If I didn't do something quickly, it would drag me under. I looked in the general direction of the football field but immediately dismissed the idea of another workout. The heat was oppressive today, and my muscles were already fatigued. I sucked in air like a drowning man and willed myself to relax. *Think, Evan, think.* I tapped my phone and Mitch's contact info popped up. I pressed Send.

"Hey, how's it going?"

"Evan?"

"Yeah. I was um...on my way to class and I found a blog you might be interested in. I forwarded the link to you. Did you see it?" I asked in a fast-paced manic tone.

Mitch didn't answer right away. I stared at the black and white checks on my Vans sneakers. The pattern blurred and sharpened. Blurred and sharpened.

"Are you okay?"

"Mmm. I think so. Just talk to me for a minute." Fuck, why didn't I call Derek? He wouldn't have required an explanation. Now I'd just made things weird with someone I really liked.

"Where are you?"

"School. I'm about to go to class. I'm late but...what about you? What are you doing?"

"I just got out of my history of film class. It's my favorite. We watch old black and white movies and then critique them. Today it was *Bringing Up Baby*. Classic screwball comedy. Silly but fun. Have you seen it?"

His voice was melodic and soothing. My pulse was beginning to steady. Five minutes or less and I'd be good to go.

"No. Tell me about it," I urged.

"Oookay, but...will you tell me what's bothering you? Is it me? Are you having second thoughts about tomorrow? 'Cause—"

"Fuck, no." I pursed my lips and sighed before continuing. "No. That's not it. Not at all. I just called to tell you about the link I sent, but I should go. I'm sorry to bug you. I—"

"I thought you wanted to hear about the movie I just saw," he intercepted playfully.

I clung to the humor in his tone with relief. "I do."

"How much time do you have?"

"Five minutes."

"All right. So the movie was released in 1938. It starred Cary Grant and Katharine Hepburn and..."

I closed my eyes and let Mitch's animated voice pull me from the proverbial wreckage with a colorful synopsis of a movie I was pretty sure I'd never see. Somehow the newness of our friendship made it easier to lean on him. If only for a little while.

THANKFULLY, I felt more like myself when class was over two hours later. My appetite returned in full force. I had a team dinner in Orange. I couldn't remember who'd asked me for a ride to the restaurant, but I figured I'd stop by the field on the way to my truck and see if anyone was waiting for me before I took off. I rounded the tall hedge by the stadium and stopped in my tracks when I spotted Jonesie standing near the entrance with a pretty brunette.

"Evan!" he called, waving me over.

I smiled at the girl as I absently exchanged fist bumps with my teammate. "Hi, Nicole. How's it going?"

"Good. I never thought I'd say this, but it's nice to be back in school. Ask me if I still feel that way during midterms," she said with a laugh.

"I know what you mean," I agreed politely.

"I'm excited about the game this weekend. You know I'm having a party after, right?"

Jonesie slapped my back and grinned. "I told him all about it. Hey, man—I gotta grab something from my locker. I'll meet you in the parking lot in a few minutes. See ya, Nicole."

Damn it. There was nothing quite like an awkward setup. I smiled tightly as I dug my keys from my pocket. "Jonesie's a smooth operator," I snarked.

Nicole threw her head back and laughed. "He's the worst. But his heart's in the right place. He told me you stuck up for me last week."

"Of course he did."

"Don't be embarrassed. I appreciate it. He doesn't mean half of the dumb things he says but...thank you."

"I didn't do anything really," I insisted.

She touched my elbow when I started to turn. I noted her long pink fingernails and her tiny wrists. She had to be a full foot shorter than me, and everything about her was petite. Her long dark hair was piled high on her head in deference to the weather and I couldn't help thinking that even her neck was small. "Come to the party, Ev."

"Uh yeah. I can't. I'll need to get back to Long Beach and—"

"You're welcome to stay the night. There's plenty of room."

Her delivery was neutral, as though she'd offer the same to anyone in need, but I heard the innuendo loud and clear.

"Thanks," I said awkwardly. "I better go or they're going to get to the food before me."

"Ha. Go on. I'll see you at the game, Evan."

My phony grin faded the second I turned toward the field. *Great.* Just what I needed.

Was it my imagination, or had my life gotten ridiculously complicated in a very short time?

MITCH HAD BEEN VERY specific about parking in the alley behind his garage, but I hadn't bothered to check out any landmarks on my previous visit. And anyone with a phobia to dark, ill-lit spaces knew it was important to have a familiar signpost or two. So I parked in front of the house like I had before and ended up in the kitchen eating cookies with Maryanne again. Chocolate chip this time.

She regaled me with a brief history lesson of my adopted

town, citing all the changes in Long Beach since she was a kid until Mitch arrived and told her we had some work to do.

"Work. Oh, is that what you kids are calling it nowadays?" Maryanne chuckled. "Go on, then. Have fun."

I followed Mitch outside with a laugh. "What does she think we're doing?"

He paused under the oak tree and gave me a funny look. "Having sex. What else?"

"Like real sex?"

"As opposed to fake sex?"

"You know what I mean. Geez, this feels weird," I grumbled, raking my hand through my hair.

Mitch chuckled. "Grow up, Evan. If she thinks we're in a relationship, she'll assume we're doing it."

"Doing what exactly?"

"How should I know? Maybe she thinks I'm gonna blow you."

"Are you?" I asked in a mock serious tone.

Mitch laughed and gave me one of his slow-moving mischievous grins. "If we can record some decent material in less than an hour, I just might."

I stared after him as he bounded up the stairs, two at a time, and adjusted my dick. I knew he was joking, but the mere thought of him on his knees with his lips around my—*oh, fuck.*

FILMING our inaugural episode seemed fairly painless after our recent conversations. Mitch set up a slick professional-looking camera on a tripod facing his kitchenette. We sat side-by-side on the barstools. I wore a black T-shirt as instructed, and Mitch wore blue. I made a crack about us looking like a bruise and was rewarded with a long explanation about the complementary palette of the entire room. Blue eyes, blue shirt, blue tea kettle on the stovetop. Black shirt, my dark eyes, and black and white photos on the wall behind us. I fixed him with a deadpan look until he busted up laughing and ran over a brief itinerary.

"The idea is to keep viewers off-balance from the start. I'll handle the intro before we launch into the questions. Feel free to jump in whenever. We'll wrap up with our dance and a quick kiss like we discussed. Sound good?"

I made a face. "I'm cool with everything but the dance."

"Oh, it'll be fun! You'll see. Just follow my lead. This isn't live TV. We can pause whenever we want. It's just easier to keep the action going. Plus it feels more natural. Ready?"

When I nodded in agreement, Mitch shifted on his barstool, clicked a button on the remote, and smiled at the camera.

"Hi, everyone. Sorry for the post delay. I've been swamped this summer with my internship, training, and general life stuff. But I'm back! I have a project to tell you about and someone special to introduce. This is Evan. He's a fifth-year senior like me. We go to different schools, but he graciously agreed to help me..."

I sat back and listened as Mitch gave a brief rundown of his project based on his own observations of social media trends in recent years. He recited data and statistics, then outlined our history and the recent changes in our relationship.

"We met through mutual friends four years ago, but we've started spending time together on our own too. We're going to ask you to join us once a week as we outline our journey. Subscribe below and please weigh in. What do you think? Is Evan really my boyfriend or is this all faux?" His dramatic intonation struck the perfect chord between playful and earnest, I mused when he paused and turned to me expectantly. "Tell everyone about your-self, hon."

"Uh..."

Mitch rolled his eyes playfully and hooked his thumb toward me. "He's camera-shy. I'll start. Evan plays football," he gushed in a campier than normal voice. "The football player and the yell leader. It's kind of delish, right?"

I snickered at his over-the-top squeal and impulsively put my arm around his shoulder. He leaned against me briefly, then sat up and got to work.

We talked for twenty minutes or more about mundane get-to-know-you topics that were supposedly meant for our audience but were helpful to me too. I didn't know Mitch started gymnastics when he was five or that he'd competed seriously in his teens. And he didn't know that my obsession with football began when I was roughly the same age.

"Do you remember what you liked about the sport when you were a kid?" he asked.

"Well, the first thing I remembered liking was the uniform," I replied with a laugh. "I got a helmet when I was four, and I used to sleep in it. My mom would come in my room at night to take it off 'cause she was afraid I'd hurt my neck. But then I loved the game. I understood the rules and what made certain players better than others. And I wanted to be one of them. I couldn't wait to join a team and wear the gear."

"What's your number?"

"Thirty-eight."

"That's my favorite number!" Mitch gasped. He snickered when I rolled my eyes and then continued. "What position do you play?"

"Fullback or tight end."

"Tight end, eh?" He waggled his brows lasciviously, then asked, "Why not quarterback? They seem to get all the love."

"That's not important to me. I just wanted to be part of something bigger than myself. There's something special about working with a bunch of guys you trust toward a common goal. Everyone is integral to the win. You gotta give it your all every time you step on the field."

Mitch nodded thoughtfully. "You're passionate about it."

"Yeah...I love it, but this is the end of the line for me. I'm hanging up my cleats after these last few games."

"Then why are you doing this with me?" His voice was low and earnest, as though my response mattered to him.

"What do you mean?"

"I'm just surprised you haven't backed out yet," he whispered.

"I'm not gonna back out. I like you," I replied.

"I like you too."

His smile brightened to something almost incandescent. He looked like a fucking angel. I nodded when he said it was time to switch the pace, but my attention span was shot. I gave automatic answers to silly questions, fixating on his bottom lip when he started talking about fruit preference. Strawberries...or maybe blueberries. I couldn't concentrate. I had a strong urge to lick the corner of his mouth and—

"Kinky or romantic?"

"Strawberries?"

Mitch chuckled. "No. We moved on."

"Oh. What's the question?"

"How do you feel at this very moment? Kinky or romantic?"

"Horny," I replied automatically.

We held each other's gaze for a moment, then busted up laughing. My answer wasn't funny. It was just...awkward. When we finally regained composure, I shifted on my stool, hooked my arm over his shoulders, and covered his mouth in a searing kiss, complete with tongue.

"Wow. Um...that was amazing." He licked his lips in a daze when he pulled back. Then he pointed at the camera. "We're supposed to dance now."

"I don't want to dance."

"But it's our boyfriend dance," he reminded me in a breathy tone.

"All right. Then dance with me, boyfriend." I reached for his hand as I stood, gently pulling him to his feet.

He stared at our laced fingers for a moment, then looked up. This time when our eyes met, we froze. I might have stopped breathing too. I couldn't tell. I set my hands on his hips and swayed from side to side in something reminiscent of a clumsy slow dance at a high school formal. It should have been silly, but it felt hopelessly...romantic. We took a turn around the island and ended up near the door.

His nostrils flared when I brushed a strand of hair from his forehead. "Are you going to kiss me again?" he whispered.

When my gaze dropped to his lips, it was all over. I swallowed hard and switched positions so fast that his head hit the door. "Fuck, I'm sorry. I—"

Mitch growled, then grabbed me around the neck and crashed his mouth over mine. The frenetic hunger in the connection surprised me. He bit my lower lip before pushing his tongue inside with a sexy moan that sent a tingle of awareness along my spine. He slipped his hands under my shirt and raked his fingernails down my back while he sucked my tongue and tilted his hips suggestively. My cock swelled in my jeans. I'd been half-hard since we'd climbed the stairs, so the added pressure against my zipper was almost painful. I needed friction badly. It didn't occur to me to second-guess what we were doing. Right now, I just wanted Mitch.

Our impromptu make-out session escalated in a flash. I grabbed his ass with both hands and ground my pelvis against his manically. Mitch gasped for air and threw his head back, hooking his leg over my thigh. I licked my way up his neck, nibbling his scruffy chin before sealing my mouth over his again. My skin tingled everywhere, and my brain was close to short-circuiting with desire. But that was okay. I didn't want to think. I just wanted to feel him. I pulled his shirt from his jeans and caressed his smooth stomach, then lowered my hand to his crotch and for the first time in my life, rubbed my palm over a man's erect cock. When he whimpered in response, I lost it. I had to have him.

I broke our feverish kiss to fumble with his belt buckle. I unbuttoned his fly and moved on to his zipper and—

"Stop."

I obeyed immediately. It took a second to string a coherent word or two together, though. I stared at his mouth before meeting his gaze. "But...don't you...?"

"Yeah, I do. In fact, the urge to get on my knees and suck your dick is pretty fucking strong."

"I'm totally okay with that," I assured him.

"If you were straight, you wouldn't like this." He grabbed my cock through my jeans and stroked. I gasped in surprise, leaning my shoulder against the door to keep from falling over.

"Fuck. That's good."

"So you *are* bi."

"I am."

"You are what?" He tightened his grip around my shaft.

"Bi," I whispered.

"Is that so hard to say?"

"Yeah. No. I—could you maybe move your hand? I'm sweating now."

Mitch pulled back and gave me a thoughtful once-over. "The camera isn't on us. No one is watching. This is real. If anything else happens between us, you can't take it back or pretend you didn't do it."

"Why would I want to?"

"Because everyone thinks you're straight, Evan. You don't want anyone to know what you want."

"I haven't lied."

"But you haven't told the truth either."

"Okay, I'm bi. It's not necessarily a secret. This is just something I don't know how to *be*. I tried once and..." I pushed unwanted memories aside and let out an aggravated rush of air. "The truth is...I don't really care about your project. I have my own shit to do, but the second you told me about this, I jumped at the chance to be close to you. I want you, Mitch. I probably have for a while, but I didn't know how to read the signs."

"What signs?" he prodded.

"Sweaty palms, fever, diarrhea..."

He gave a reluctant half laugh and then pursed his lips. "Sounds serious."

"It is. Now you know my secrets. I'm bi, I like you, and I'm very inexperienced at anything remotely romantic so...I should probably go and—"

"Stay." Mitch put his hand on my arm.

"And then what?"

"Tell me what you want from me."

I swallowed hard. "I want to be with you. Talk to you, kiss you..."

"I thought you wanted me to suck your dick?"

I couldn't tell if he was playing with me now or if he was serious, but I nodded like a puppet and went with honesty. "I do."

"Then don't go. Let me see you."

My fingers shook as I obeyed, fumbling with my belt and undoing my fly before finally unzipping. I pulled my T-shirt over my head, then hooked my thumbs at my waist. His gaze roamed up and down my chest. Some weird part of me wanted to flex my muscles to impress him, but I needed him to direct us. I couldn't do this on my own.

"Should I...do you want me to take my jeans off?" I croaked.

"Yes," he replied in a sex-hazed tone.

Thank fuck. My rigid cock sprang forward as I shoved the fabric over my ass and down my legs. I grabbed myself at the base and stroked. I'd never done this in front of another guy. Ever. And apparently I'd been missing out. Mitch's slack-jawed admiring stare was good for my confidence. The longer I stood jacking myself languidly with my jeans pooled at my ankles, the more sure I felt. This was right and good. But it could be better.

"Come here. Touch me."

He stepped between my legs and licked his lips hungrily before wrapping his fingers around me. I hissed at the contact. His hand was warm, and his firm grip felt like a velvet glove. When he squeezed my length and swiped his thumb across my slit, I shivered with need. He let go for a moment to free himself from his jeans and toss his T-shirt over his shoulder. Then he flattened his chest against mine and tilted his hips. The immediate zing of pleasure was intense. I glanced down at us in wonder. His cock was beautiful. He was smaller than me, but not by much. And he looked thick too. I reached down without thinking and gripped both of us in one hand.

"Fuck, that feels so good," he purred, setting his hand over mine.

Good was too weak an adjective. He felt incredible. It wouldn't take much to come now, I mused as I captured his mouth in a searing kiss. We stood there locked in a passionate tangle, stroking each other as we licked and sucked, only surfacing to gasp for air.

"Oh God, I'm close," I moaned.

"No. Wait," he commanded before sinking to his knees.

He looked up at me then and licked his swollen lips before swallowing me whole. He pulled back to lick me from base to tip while he jacked himself with his right hand. Then he twirled his tongue around the wide mushroom head before sucking as much of me as he could at once. My breath caught in my throat. I couldn't believe this was happening. What had he said earlier? The cheerleader and the football player. It was like a dream come true to have a sexy yell leader sucking my cock, kneading my balls, and brushing his fingers over my hole and—*oh fuck.*

My orgasm hit me like a bolt of lightning. I pushed at his forehead, but I couldn't speak to warn him. Mitch didn't seem to mind, though. He sucked harder, milking me dry before sitting back on his heels just as his release shot into the air. I laughed when he wiped at his chin with the back of his hand.

"Leave it. I'll help you," I said.

I offered him my hand and pulled him against me, cupping his ass to hold him close before crashing my mouth over his. He tasted like me now. Like he was part of me. Or like he should be part of me.

We made out in a passionate tangle of tongues and roving hands that was sweet and sexy and promising. After a few minutes, I kissed his nose and cradled his chin to get a good look at him.

"That was fucking incredible."

"Are you okay? You're not gonna hate me in the morning, are you?" he asked.

"Not a chance." I traced his jaw and smiled softly. "Who are we now? Do we have a new title or something?"

Mitch captured my hand and kissed my knuckles. "Nothing changes, silly. We're still just friends."

I wanted to argue that I didn't fuck around with my friends, but he was right. One blowjob didn't make a new relationship.

"Okay. I'll follow your lead. I don't know what to do or how to act. If I fuck up, tell me and I'll—"

"Hey." Mitch squeezed my hand as he held my gaze meaningfully. "You don't have to do anything or act a certain way. Just be you. I'll be me and we'll see where we land."

I nodded in agreement and then asked, "We're not talking about this in the video, right?"

"Hell no! That's...not real. It's just a project."

"Right. Well..." I bent to pull my jeans and briefs up, then leaned in to kiss him. "For what it's worth, I think it's going to be amazing."

"Me too."

Maybe the significance of what we'd done would hit me later. Maybe I'd feel altered somehow and different in my own skin. I couldn't say, but I knew I wouldn't change a thing.

5

In the following days, I was grateful that Mitch was a good texter. Mindless back and forth conversations about our classes and friends helped ease the awkwardness I feared would set in after our impromptu blowjob-against-the-door. But it wasn't enough. I needed to see him and yeah, I wanted to touch him again. I didn't want to wait a week to film a video I had zero interest in.

I thought about asking him out, but I didn't know if that was overstepping an imaginary boundary. Even if it was okay, I didn't know how to do it. A simple "Do you want to go to dinner?" seemed like a very hard question to ask. The problem was...doing nothing was driving me insane. After three days, I gave in and texted him before my second practice.

Hi. Do you want to

I pushed Send before I finished my sentence and stared at my screen in a panic. Now what?

Mitch immediately replied.

Do I want to...what?

The instant shortness of breath alarmed me. Oh no. I couldn't think that fast. I had to call him.

"Hi."

"Hi. What's up, Ev? Are you—"

"What are you doing tonight?" I blurted, nodding at one of my teammates before stepping away from the door to the locker room.

"Um...laundry, homework. Oh yeah, and I have to go to Target."

"Hmm. Busy guy. Want company? I should be home around seven. If you're free or just doing laundry, maybe we could hang out."

I squeezed my eyes shut, wincing at the flood of lameness spouting from my mouth. I sounded desperate and a tad obsessive. Not cool at all.

"Just hang out," he repeated. "This wouldn't have anything to do with the other night or—"

"No! Well, yeah, but not in a creepy way." I licked my lips nervously and paced a few yards away before continuing. "I'm not looking for a booty call. I just want..."

"What do you want, Evan?" he prodded gently.

"To be with you. That's all."

I held my breath and waited for his version of a gentle rejection. I couldn't believe how nervous I felt. My hands were slick, and my knees felt rubbery. This couldn't be good for me.

"Okay," he said after what felt like ten minutes but was probably two seconds. "What time?"

"I can pick you up at seven," I said in a rush.

"It's a date."

"Great. So, just to clarify...is this a Target date, or can I take you to dinner?"

"You want to take me to dinner?"

"Well, yeah. They have a concession stand there. We can grab pizza, slushies..."

Mitch's laughter floated between us. The joyful sound chased the butterflies in my stomach away and left me feeling calm...and happy.

"We can play it by ear, big spender. I'll see you tonight."

A FEW HOURS LATER, I was in a mini version of hell. Not that I had a thing against Target or any place where you could simultaneously buy bananas and bicycles. But it was busier than I anticipated, and following the guy I had a crush on down congested aisles stacked high with consumer goods was frustrating. I stared at his ass as I pushed the cart a few paces behind him. He looked hot tonight, I mused. His snug designer jeans hugged his ass in all the right places and went well with his unicorn "Sounds gay, count me in" T-shirt. He'd fixed me with a challenging look as though daring me to comment when I'd picked him up. I'd wisely complimented him and asked for directions instead.

"How much more do you have to get?" I grumbled, setting a proprietary hand on our red cart when a fellow shopper bumped into it.

Mitch checked his list. And maybe it was wishful thinking, but he seemed to lean in a little closer than the average guy hangin' out with a buddy would. He brushed his fingers against my forearm, sending a shiver along my spine.

"Three more things. Toilet paper, detergent, and toothpaste."

"And candy. I'm in the mood for a jumbo pack of peanut M&Ms," I declared.

"That's not good for you."

"I had an intense workout this afternoon. I gotta treat myself. What kind do you want? I'm buyin'."

"Thanks, but I don't want candy."

"Do you want flowers?" I asked.

He glanced up at me in surprise and chuckled. "Well, not right this second, but I like flowers. Who doesn't?"

"What's your favorite kind?"

"Hmm. Tough question. Peonies. I like hydrangeas too."

"Any particular color?"

"Pink."

"Why pink?" I asked, moving our cart to make room for a passing shopper.

"I don't know. I just like it. Light or dark. When I was a kid, my first-grade teacher went around the classroom asking everyone what their favorite color was. At first I couldn't wait to answer. I held my hand up like everyone else, but she went by row and gave everyone a chance. There were all kinds of answers...red, blue, purple. But only the girls said they liked pink. When it was finally my turn, I lost my nerve."

"What'd you say?"

"Blue, I think. Not a total lie but...it wasn't my favorite. And I have no idea why I just told you that story," he said with a laugh.

" 'Cause you want me to buy you pink flowers."

"No, I don't," he protested as he studied the stack of toilet paper.

"You know, I thought about buying you flowers tonight," I admitted. "I should have."

"Why?" he asked with a laugh. His eyes crinkled at the sides, and his cheeks turned red.

"We're on a date. You're supposed to bring flowers or candy or something, aren't you? But flowers and Target..." I made a face and shrugged. "It's a weird combo."

"This isn't a date, Evan. It's a necessary shopping trip." He corrected me before reaching for a jumbo package of toilet paper on the top shelf.

I pulled it down for him and held it above my head.

"What about candy? What's your favorite kind? Come on," I coaxed. "First one that pops into your head."

"This may shock you, but I really don't know," he replied stubbornly.

"Then let's go candy shopping." I slipped my left hand into his and pushed the cart with my right one.

Mitch tugged at my fingers but gave in and let me lead the way, shaking his head in mock dismay when we reached our destination. "Really?"

"Oh yeah. What's it gonna be, baby? King Size Reese's, Junior Mints, Hershey's Kisses...your wish is my command."

His sweet grin grew to epic proportions until it covered his face in a megawatt smile that felt like sunshine and moonbeams. I wanted to offer so much more than a measly bag of candy in that moment, but I wasn't sure where to begin.

"Do you have a suggestion?" he asked, biting his bottom lip.

"When in doubt, M&Ms. They never let you down," I assured him in a serious tone as I picked up a packet of peanut ones.

"Okay. But I'll get plain. Then we'll have one of each." He grabbed a small bag and tossed it into the cart.

"Good thinking, except...we go big." I returned his bag to the shelf and replaced it with one four times the size.

Mitch chuckled indulgently and kissed my cheek. "Thanks."

"You're welcome. Oh hey!" I spied a display of Good & Plentys and hurried over to grab a box before presenting it to him like a rare and special prize. "Ta da! They're pink."

I didn't think it was possible, but his smile widened. He giggled like a kid and nodded, tapping the box of licorice candies. "Yes, they're very pink. And white."

"We're all about the pink ones today." I shook the contents then ripped open the top.

"Evan! What are you doing? They're going to kick us out!"

"Don't worry. I'm buying these. Just...put your hands out," I instructed.

Mitch gave me a quizzical look but obeyed. I dropped a few candies onto his palms and picked out the white ones, leaving the pink for him.

"Now what?"

"Eat 'em."

He popped the pink candy-coated licorice in his mouth and grinned. "Thank you. Pink is definitely the best."

I chomped on a white Good & Plenty and made a face. "These things suck."

Mitch snickered. "You know, we can do a taste test on our next video. Plain or peanut M&Ms or—"

"No."

"Why not?"

" 'Cause this is just for us. I know this isn't anything special but—"

"Yes, it is. It's very special. No one's ever bought me pink candy before. Thank you."

I scanned the aisle. A lady decked in executive office wear shot an inquisitive glance our way. It wasn't judgmental. Just curious. I'd never been in a position where a stranger might openly wonder about my sexual orientation. Ever. Maybe a couple of patrons at The Grill gave us a second look when I kissed him, but that was for the project. I'd practically been auditioning that day. This was just...us. Two guys milling the aisles on a quest for basic crap everyone needs. No agenda. No plan.

There was a time the very notion of anyone suspecting I was different would have freaked me out. Football players weren't gay. Football players were tough and strong. And they went out with hot babes. Not effeminate guys who wore unicorn shirts and made them push the cart at a crowded store.

Yet here I was. And I liked it. No, I loved it. He made my heart skip a beat, but in a good way.

"I think you should kiss me. A pound of chocolate and a box of licorice candy is worth at least one kiss."

"Here?" he asked.

"Right here. Right now."

Mitch smiled and fuck, he looked pretty. He stepped closer and pressed his lips against mine. I snaked my arm around his waist and deepened the connection. It wasn't an overly passionate kiss, but it felt significant. Kissing for no particular reason was something lovers did all the time; however, I didn't see many guys locking lips in public. It seemed to take an act of bravery for gay couples to be seen holding hands or showing any affection toward each other. I'd always thought of myself as being tougher than the norm, but I was beginning to realize I had nothing on this guy.

We stepped back and stared at each other for a long moment. I sensed a change in us. A beginning. And yeah, it scared me a little. I felt like I was running onto a field without a helmet and had no idea what I was up against. But damn, it felt good.

MOST PEOPLE DESCRIBED me as a mild-mannered goofball. That was only partially true. My parents were brainiacs, and they had big expectations for my brother and me. I might not be an astrophysicist in the making, but I'd be okay once I figured out what I wanted to do with my life. I'd always been that way. Once something caught my attention, I was all in. That was how football was for me. My game-day mindset was about focus. I tried to keep social interaction to a minimum. I didn't like to talk too much or overexert myself. Light cardio in the morning, a healthy breakfast, and a day spent watching football highlights and listening to upbeat jams helped me mentally prepare for the game. Usually.

I checked my cell for the umpteenth time before our quarterback revved up for his pre-game rah-rah speech. I spotted Christian pacing next to the lockers, bopping his head manically as he picked up steam. I had a message from my mom letting me know they were in the stands, and one from Nicole, reminding me about another post-game party she was hosting. Damn, that girl had a lot of parties, I mused. How did she get my number? Oh, yeah. I cast an irritated glance at Jonesie stretching his hamstrings a few feet away and was about to put my phone in my bag when a new message lit up my screen.

Our last video turned out amazing. I pieced together fifteen minutes of awesomeness. I'll send you the link when I get home. Check it out and give me a thumbs up if you're okay with me posting as is.

I typed a quick response. *I'll come over after my game. We can watch it together.*

Ok. I'll be home after eleven. See you later.

I should have put my cell away then, but I stared at my phone with a stupid smile on my mug, hoping he'd add something more. Was a simple, "Yes, I like you too and I've been thinking about sucking your dick all day" too much to ask?

Maybe I should have been alarmed by how often I'd thought about him. Maybe we weren't boyfriends, but we were something more than we intended. I followed his lead like I said I would, hoping it meant he'd want to continue where we left off. Thankfully, he did.

We used his project as an excuse to get to know each other on and off camera. I'd seen a private side of him he hadn't intended to show me. He was genuine and sweet. There was something calming and kind in his mannerisms that fascinated me. And something about his body that made me horny twenty-four seven.

I couldn't help it. I thought about sex constantly. I loved touching him and yeah, I loved his mouth on my dick, but I felt paralyzed by my inexperience sometimes. There were so many more things I wanted to do—like suck him...I just didn't know how to ask. Every time I thought about it, I ended up jacking off. In fact, I'd jerked off more in the past couple of weeks than I had all summer. No joke. My usual guy-on-girl-on-guy porn didn't do it for me, though. The thought of cupping Mitch's ass and grinding my dick against his pelvis was enough to push me over the edge. But I had to keep my overactive libido in check. I had a game to play and a party to avoid before anything else happened.

"Hey, di Angelo, we're huddling here! What the fuck are you looking at?" Jonesie swiped my phone from my hand and held it above his head.

And I reacted like anyone with possibly incriminating texts on their cell would....I lunged for his throat and held him against the locker in a chokehold. Three guys were on me in a flash. Christian grabbed my phone from Jonesie and scowled.

"Jesus, Evan!" He took a peek at my cell before handing it back to me. "What's the big deal? You like Nicole and she doesn't seem to think you're a total asshole. I shoulda known this was about a girl."

The room broke into a round of obnoxious catcalls and wolf whistles that were more about restoring order than taunting. I glanced at the screen before tossing my phone into the bag in my locker. Yep, it was Nicole. I fussed with my shoulder pads when Jonesie sidled up next to me, extending his hand in a conciliatory fist bump while Christian called the team into a huddle.

"You have a fucking rotten temper," he huffed.

"I do. So stay the fuck away from my cell, asswipe." I pulled my helmet over my head and fastened the strap.

"Fine! Geez! But you should be thanking me for making things happen with Nicole. I expect an invitation to your wedding," Jonesie said sarcastically as he dealt with his own helmet.

This was what I'd meant when I told Mitch people believed what they wanted. Even if I corrected Jonesie, he wouldn't buy that I'd been mooning over a text from another guy.

I pulled Jonesie's face mask and gave him a lazy grin. "Don't dry clean your tux yet, buddy. It's not about a girl, it's about a guy."

Jonesie's frown morphed into a shit-eating grin. He busted up laughing, then slapped me on the back. "Right. Maybe I should tell Nicole you're a 'mo."

"Tell her what you want."

He furrowed his brow and was about to speak when Christian called us over. "Kiss and make up already, you two. Let's go!"

"We're coming. Evan was just coming out to me." He dodged sideways to avoid certain retaliation.

I ignored him and smiled as the room erupted in another round of laughter. They could think what they wanted. They always would. But it occurred to me that I'd done something I never had before. I'd said the words aloud. It didn't matter if they believed me tonight. Someday they would. I'd make sure of it.

WE WON BY A LANDSLIDE. The final score was twenty-one to three. The Mavericks were up by three on a field goal kick at the half, but the tide changed in the third quarter. Christian handed me the ball on the second play and *boom*...I ran forty-five yards into the end zone for our first goal. The rest was a walk in the park.

Everyone was in a celebratory mood after the game. Someone turned on a JT song, and we danced and goofed off while we cleaned up before meeting with the family and friends who'd stayed to congratulate us. I greeted my parents with big hugs, and because they caught me in a weak moment, I agreed to come home the next night for dinner. As we chatted about the game, I found myself checking the stands, wishing I'd thought to invite Mitch.

"Hey, can I get a ride with you to that party?" Christian asked, yanking at my jersey as we headed off the field.

"I wasn't planning on going."

"Do me a huge favor and come with me for half an hour."

"Why?"

"I promised I'd stop by, and I was specifically asked to bring you. We don't have to stay long. Thirty minutes, an hour, tops. I'll get a ride from there. What do you say?"

I didn't bother asking who requested my presence. I sighed

heavily and checked the time on the giant stadium clock. Nine forty-five. Mitch wouldn't even be home for an hour.

"Okay."

Christian slapped my back and grinned. "Cool. I owe you one."

ATHLETES SEEMED to roll into parties with an entourage and a lot of fanfare. Especially when they were in season. Some of the guys on my team acted like every post-win event was a personal congratulations and an occasion to celebrate to excess. Not everyone, of course. Christian might have one drink, but he'd manage to nurse it for an hour or more. Jonesie, on the other hand, would waltz into Nicole's house with his arms in the air, then make a beeline to the keg. He'd guzzle three beers before making his rounds, flirting and goofing around with friends and teammates. By the end of the night, he'd be leaning against a wall for support with his arm over an adoring girl's shoulder.

I was somewhere in between. I liked a good time as much as the next guy, but I didn't like being hungover. I knew my limits and I stuck to them. But when I was twenty minutes away from home by car, I'd have to crash on someone's couch. Not tonight. I sipped soda water from a red cup and fake smiled as one of my teammates told a lame-ass story involving super human powers that would have seemed impressive if I was drunk. I wasn't. And after forty minutes, I was ready to go.

Unfortunately, it wouldn't be easy. Nicole had been glued to my side since I walked in the door. I couldn't talk freely with anyone else, and I hadn't been able to check my phone without her staring over my shoulder. And unfortunately, this wasn't the time or place to tell her I wasn't interested. She was tipsy and there were far too many people around. It would have to wait. If I couldn't fade gracefully, I'd have to make an excuse and get the fuck out.

I chuckled on cue and dropped my arm, gently dislodging Nicole's hand from my bicep. I set my cup on an end table and stepped aside to pull my cell from my pocket.

" 'Scuse me. I have to return this call."

I held up my phone as though it was proof of my sincerity. Then I slipped through the crowded living room into the hallway near the front door. I thought about just leaving, but there were too many people lingering in the area to make a clean getaway. This worked, I mused as I pushed Call.

Mitch answered on the first ring. "Why are you calling me?"

"You're supposed to say hello," I chided.

"Hello. Why are you calling?"

I let out my first honest-to-God laugh of the night and stepped farther into the shadows. "I missed you. Why else?"

"Yeah, right," he snarked. "Are you drunk?"

"No, but everyone else here is. I'm sipping soda water at a college party, wishing I was at home watching Sports Center in my underwear. When did I get so old? Everyone here looks so peppy and pretty and...it's kinda creepy, ya know?"

"Wow. You really do miss me," he teased.

"I'm one of those painfully honest guys, Mitch. Ask Derek."

"Hmm. I saw him at Chelsea's party tonight with some water polo hotties."

"You're at a party too?" I asked. "Seems quiet in the background."

"I'm home. It's almost eleven. Are you still coming over?"

"Yeah. I'm on my way."

I smiled as I disconnected the call and moved into the light. And immediately ran into my hostess.

"Oh, there you are! I hoped I didn't scare you away," Nicole said in a sultry tone.

"No, I'm...here. But I have to go." I sidestepped around her but didn't get far.

She blocked my way and struck a pose against the doorjamb. "Don't go."

"Sorry, but someone's waiting for me."

"A girl?"

"No."

"Good. I try to be very respectful of relationships. But I know you don't have a girlfriend," she said with a Cheshire cat grin. "Jonesie told me you were single but besides that, we have mutual friends in Long Beach. I went to high school with Amanda."

"She mentioned that," I replied blandly.

Nicole lowered her lashes then moved from the wall and placed her hand on my hip. She played with the collar of my shirt, stealthily undoing a button before I caught her wrist.

"I've never told you this, but I've had a crush on you for a while, Evan. You were in a few group pics Amanda had online back when she and Derek were together. I couldn't believe we went to the same school. I was too nervous to introduce myself, but I watched your games and...I like you. That's all."

She gripped the back of my neck and kissed my throat, licking a path along my Adam's apple as her hand drifted to my crotch.

Okay. *Wow.* Well, I could honestly say no one had ever pursued me quite so enthusiastically in a long time. Nicole was sweet and pretty, and I hadn't been with a girl in forever. My epic libido alone should have steered me straight. Pun intended. And though I was flattered, I wasn't interested, which was hard to explain without being painfully honest.

I grabbed her hand and shook my head. "Sorry. I can't. I—I *am* seeing someone."

"You are?" she asked in bewilderment.

"It's new and I don't want to mess anything up."

"Oh. Do I know her?"

I squinted as though the gesture might help me understand

the question. This was a "coming out" moment, but it wasn't the one I wanted. There was no way I'd tell a girl I barely knew about the guy I liked before I told my family and my best friends. So I took the easy way out.

"No. I don't think so. Um...I should go. I'll see you at school."

She reached for my wrist and sidled close again. "If it's new, I'm going to assume I still have a chance. Call me if something changes."

I kissed her cheek before I left, which in retrospect might have been a mistake. In my mind, I wasn't sending mixed signals. I was just relieved I'd said what I needed to, and I thought I'd been fairly clear. Not bad, considering I was completely out of my depth. I didn't know how to tell a girl I wanted a guy.

THE ALLEY behind Mitch's garage was dark and narrow. I didn't do well with dark and narrow. I paused to wipe my slick palms on my jeans and give myself a quick pep talk before slowly turning onto what felt like the initial part of a scary as fuck ride at an amusement park. Or a rotten trip down memory lane. My heart beat like a jackhammer and sweat beaded my forehead halfway in. I fully intended to circle around, park on the street and tiptoe through the side gate to get to his place. But then I spotted Mitch waiting for me and just like that, I could breathe again.

He gestured for me to pull up in front of the garage door. I obeyed, swiped my damp palms on my thighs one last time, and jumped out of my SUV.

"Hi! You made good ti—*oomph!*"

I pulled him against me and held on tight. I wasn't in a hurry to move, but when he stepped backward and reached for my hand, I followed him along the unlit pathway to the stairs leading to his studio above the garage.

"You okay?" he asked when we stepped inside.

"I'm fine. Just...happy to be here."

Mitch considered me for a moment, then filled a glass with water and set it on the island. He grabbed a blue sports drink from his mini refrigerator and held it up. "I have blue or orange. Which one?"

"Neither. Water is good."

"You should replenish your electrolytes after a game," he scolded lightly.

"Thanks, Doc, but I've had plenty of that stuff today. Besides, everyone knows red is the best."

"Diva."

That made me laugh. "Dude. I am no one's idea of a diva. Look at me."

I spread my arms wide and tried to keep a straight face when Mitch waltzed toward me, tapping his fingers against his chin thoughtfully as he fixed me with a thorough once-over.

"Hmm. Basic denim, scuffed Nikes, and a blue and white button-down with a lipstick stain on your collar. You're right. Not diva material at all. You look like a regular guy on the prowl on a Saturday night. Which makes me wonder...what are you doing here with me?"

"I'm here to prowl on you. And I don't have lipstick..." I undid the top few buttons on my shirt and pulled at my collar to get a glimpse of any possible lipstick marks. "Where is it?"

"Right there." He stepped into my space and pointed at the pink smudge on my shirt. "What's her name?"

"Nicole. She's after me. Help," I pleaded pathetically.

Mitch snickered. "Poor guy. First Amanda, now Nicole."

I huffed humorlessly. "They're friends."

"Yeah, I remember. Chelsea's party," he added when I gave him a curious look.

"Right. I can't decide if it's a small world or a weird one."

"It's not *that* weird. Orange and Long Beach aren't far apart. I know a lot of people at your school too. The first guy I ever blew goes there."

"Good to know," I snarked.

"Besides, you're a hot football player. An awfully popular one too, so it seems."

"Hmph. I don't know about that." I studied a knife mark on the island's butcher block surface before meeting his gaze. "I told her I was seeing someone."

"You did?"

"Yeah. I mean...we are seeing each other, right?" I furrowed my brow as I sat back, noting his light-pink T-shirt and matching striped pajama bottoms. The color looked good on him. It complemented his golden hair and skin. Damn, he was pretty.

He regarded me thoughtfully and nodded. "Yes."

I grinned. One of those mega grins that actually hurts your face after a few seconds. Then I reached for his hand and laced my fingers with his.

"Cool," I said lamely.

Mitch huffed a laugh then let go of my hand and skirted the island. He gave me a bashful smile as he perched on the barstool next to me. "So I'm guessing the lipstick came before your declaration?"

"Exactly. I fought her off like a ninja warrior." I supplied a couple of ninja-style moves complete with sound effects before adding, "And then I told her about you."

"Me specifically?" It was a rhetorical question; he knew the answer.

"No," I admitted.

"Oh."

Suddenly, I felt small next to him. Ordinary. I'd kicked ass on the football field and contributed to an important win tonight and then told a girl who liked me I was "seeing someone" as though that was another high achievement. My earlier feeling of accomplishment faded fast. I wasn't so strong or brave after all. Nothing like him.

"I should have," I said.

"Hey, don't beat yourself up. You'll get there in your own time."

I nodded absently. "I wish I was there now. I wish it was easy."

"Nothing worthwhile is easy."

"Trust me, my life is one hundred percent easier letting everyone think I'm just like them," I scoffed.

"Evan, you're the same guy who said sex is sex and love is love. It's no one's business who you sleep with, so why do you care what they think?"

"I don't." I took a deep breath and looked away for a moment. "I'll get there, Mitch. Just give me some time."

"There's no pressure. I mean it. I'm okay with this for now. I like having you around. You're silly and sweet and you make me laugh. This is good."

I wanted to take exception with the "for now" disclaimer but I was sure I wouldn't like what he had to say, so I switched gears. I rubbed the inside of his thigh and gave him a curious look.

"You know, technically we're sleeping together minus the sleepover part. We should have one of those."

"We should."

"Yes, we should. And just to be clear, "sleepover" is code, right?"

Mitch threw his head back and laughed. "What kind of code?"

"Sex code," I said in a raspier than normal voice.

Mitch's hungry stare chased away the last of my demons. I ached to touch him...his hair, his lips, his throat. But I needed him to lead. I held my breath and waited for him to say something or do something.

He inclined his head and moved to his bed. He slipped his

shoes off, fluffed his pillow, lay back, and patted the space next to him.

"What are you waiting for?"

"Uh...okay. Do you want me to take something off?" I asked, fumbling with my belt buckle.

"Start with your shoes."

"Right."

I kicked off my sneakers, then sank back on the pillow and stealthily leaned against him, so we were shoulder to shoulder. A new jolt of electricity sent a shockwave down my arm, through my chest, and landed squarely on my crotch. My dick swelled in my jeans.

I sucked in a deep breath and tried to relax. His hair and skin smelled delicious, like springtime rain and maybe strawberries. No, that was weird. Guys didn't smell like strawberries. Maybe it was lotion. He must have just gotten out of the shower. I bent my head slightly and sniffed his T-shirt. I liked the contrast of his lean, toned muscles next to my bigger biceps. We looked good next to each other. Hot, even. When the corner of his mouth lifted in a slow, wicked grin, I met his gaze and gulped.

"You're staring at me," he said softly.

"I know. I want you so bad, but...I don't want to make you uncomfortable if I roll on top of you and kiss the fuck out of you."

"I'd be okay with that. You look kind of intense right now. What if things go further than you wanted? Are you sure you—"

I grabbed his wrist and molded his palm over my throbbing cock. "I feel pretty sure. But maybe you should get on top and show me what to do."

"I can do that. What do you want first? Should I suck you?"

I smiled at the challenge in his voice. He was testing me. And though I understood, I wanted to assure him there was no need for caution. I wasn't going anywhere. My mind was open, and my body was more than willing.

"Do it," I said in a low raspy voice as he unbuckled my belt. "And if you feel like riding my cock, I'm okay with that too, baby."

Mitch stilled his hand and sat up suddenly. He scooted between my legs and motioned for me to unbutton my shirt. I obeyed, holding his gaze while he unzipped my jeans. He pushed the denim aside, revealing my impressive bulge in my precum-soaked black boxer briefs. He hummed his approval as he leaned back to stroke his shaft through his Pjs.

"You want to fuck me?" he purred.

My mouth instantly went dry. I licked my lips and nodded profusely. "Yeah, I do."

He shivered in response and then pushed his pajama bottoms and briefs down and yanked his tee over his head. He motioned for me to get naked too, scooting sideways to give me room to maneuver. I sat up and shrugged my shirt off then lay back again to shuck my jeans down my legs. Mitch knelt in the middle of the bed to help me. I drank in the sight of his toned muscular body as he moved above me. And when he straddled my thighs, settling his bare ass over my painfully erect dick, I bit my lip and tried not to whimper.

I glanced up to meet his gaze and reached for his cock. He let out a sweet-sounding groan when I tightened my grip and stroked. Then I reached behind him and traced his crack. He wiggled at the featherlight contact and shifted so I could grab myself with my left hand while I worked him over with my right.

Mitch let me explore at my own pace for a while. His soft moans of approval gave me the confidence to squeeze harder and pick up the tempo. I brushed the precum from his slit down his length to use for lube. When that didn't seem like enough, I let go of him and spit on my hand, then gripped him again and stroked a little harder.

"Is that okay? Or do you want me to use the real thing?"

He chuckled. "By 'real thing,' do you mean, use your mouth?"

I smacked his ass and gestured for him to slide up my chest. "Closer. Put your dick in my mouth."

His eyes widened in surprise, but he didn't ask questions. He scrambled close and set the tip of his cock on my bottom lip. I licked at the precum on his slit, then propped my head higher on the pillow and bent to suck him.

"Oh, my God."

My vision blurred, and my body tingled all over. This had to be the sexiest thing I'd ever done. And if Mitch's purr of pleasure and the tilt of his hips was any indication, I wasn't doing a bad job. I held him at the base and licked one side, then the other, before trying to suck a little more. I bobbed my head experimentally as I upped the tempo, jacking my cock in rhythmic unison. He chanted my name and yanked my hair as he writhed over me wantonly. But then he pushed at my forehead until I released him and slid down my chest, panting for air.

"What's wrong?"

"Everything is perfect, Ev. But I want to try something else."

He leaned over to grab a condom and a bottle of lube from his nightstand drawer and dropped them next to me. Then he straddled my torso and licked my lips as he stared into my eyes.

"You're trying to tell me something," I whispered.

"Yeah. I'm going to suck your cock, and it's going to drive you crazy." He swayed his hips enticingly as he bent to flick his tongue over my right nipple and then my left before continuing south. "You'll want to fuck me and—"

"That might not be possible. I'm gonna fuckin' explode if you keep that up," I groaned.

"Try to hang on. I'm worth it." Mitch flashed a mischievous grin at me and then winked before swallowing me whole.

And damn, he knew what he was doing. Mitch hollowed his cheeks on one side to take as much of me as possible, then alternately sucked and licked while he played with my balls and traced my crack. When I put my hand over his head to keep him in place, he hummed and that was almost the end for me. But he pulled away and reached for the lube and condom.

"What do you want to do now?"

"Do I get choices? 'Cause you gotta know I have no idea what to do," I said in a huskier than normal tone.

"I don't believe you."

"Why not?" I wasn't sure why I asked. I guess it seemed like something that should bug me.

"I can tell you know what you're doing. At least a little bit." He set the condom on my stomach and uncapped the lube. Then he poured the gel into his palm, slathered two fingers on his right hand, and reached back.

"Are you? Wh—where are your fingers?"

"In my ass," he finished with a smirk.

"That's what I want. Your ass."

"Hurry up. Put the condom on."

I fumbled with the wrapper but finally managed to open it and slide the latex over my impossibly hard cock while he stretched his hole. His lithe movement and unabashed confidence were a heady combination. I held my breath when he reached for a tissue from his nightstand to wipe the lube off. His precum trailed across my lower abdomen. I ran a finger through it and waited for him to look at me before licking it clean.

His eyes took on a sex-hazed expression that let me know he was as strung out as me. For some reason that was the reassurance I needed.

"C'mere. Kiss me," I commanded.

Mitch propped his hands on either side of my head and sealed his mouth over mine. Our tongues twisted sensuously for a long moment. Then he broke for air and inched backward until my sheathed cock slid against his crack. He held eye contact as he positioned me at his entrance.

He bit his bottom lip as he braced one hand on my chest and then slowly lowered himself onto me. I wished there was a way to float above and watch what we were doing and still experience the sensation of slowly joining our bodies. It was...unreal. Amazing.

He was warm and tight and so unbelievably beautiful. The urge to buck my hips and plunge inside him in one fell swoop was strong, but I paid close attention to his expression and followed his lead. Mitch closed his eyes and winced, then pulled off and tried again. I massaged his thighs and held my breath. This time he didn't stop until he'd taken every inch of me.

"You're bigger than I thought," he said with a laugh.

"Does it hurt?"

"A little. But it's getting better. Just give me a second. How does it feel to you?"

I opened my mouth and closed it twice. I didn't have words to describe this, but I had to find them. He should know how incredible he was.

"Perfect," I whispered reverently. "You look so beautiful. Your hair, your eyes, and you feel tight but not too tight. Just really fucking perfect. I want to tell you I love you right now. Is it too soon?"

Mitch threw his head back and laughed. "You're an idiot. You don't love me, but"—he rolled his hips back and forth experimentally—"I'm gonna make you wish you did. Are you ready?"

"Fuck, yes. Tell me what to do." My voice sounded strangled, like he had his hands around my throat.

He squeezed my tits as he continued a tentative rocking motion. "Grab my ass. Mmm. That's good. Now tilt your hips and...*oh, fuck.* Yes. I'm gonna ride you."

Those four words strung together in his husky, lust-filled tone were nearly my undoing. And we'd barely begun. I gritted my teeth and hoped like hell I could keep my cool and not embarrass myself by coming from a little dirty talk. No, I had to act like I knew what the hell I was doing here.

I gripped his ass cheeks and gave him a roguish smile. "Do it, cowboy."

Mitch snickered appreciatively and began to move. He set a moderate pace at first, curling his toes around my knees for purchase as he rode my cock, lifting himself up and down like a pro. He stroked himself rhythmically and lowered his eyelids. His blissed-out expression was its own kind of aphrodisiac. I'd never been this turned-on from watching my lover. His obvious pleasure gave me confidence. I wanted to make him feel even better.

I flattened my feet on the mattress and bucked my hips. My balls slapped his ass obscenely and fuck, that was kinda hot. Mitch agreed.

"Oh, yes. That's good. More," he said.

He upped the tempo and so did I. We moved in perfect unison. When he lost his stride, I held his hips firmly and pistoned upward over and over. He groaned and chanted my name as he stroked himself so fast I could hardly see his fingers. I couldn't tell for sure, but he seemed close and I didn't want him to come yet.

"Stop."

I gestured for him to bend toward me. He obeyed immediately. I bucked my hips as I traced his Adam's apple. Then I cupped his neck and sealed my mouth over his. The passionate fusion of tongues and bodies were a perfect complement to the sound of heavy breathing and squeaky bedsprings. I wrapped my arms around him and shifted sideways before rolling on top of him, never breaking the kiss.

Mitch hiked his legs and rested them on my lower back, then wiggled his ass meaningfully. He didn't have to say a word. I knew exactly what he wanted.

I bit his lower lip and rose above him, setting one hand on the headboard and the other on his shoulder. We stared at each other in silent communication. He was giving me the reins and permission to take over and do whatever the fuck I wanted. I grinned down at him and quickened my pace. I pistoned my hips and fucked him relentlessly. Mitch slipped one hand between us to jack his cock, alternately tracing my crack and gripping my ass cheek with the other. Every sigh and gasp of desire spurred me on. Wave upon wave of pleasure built steadily. I couldn't hold on much longer. And when he froze in my arms and cried my name as his release spurted between us, I was right there with him.

Here's the thing about orgasms...I'd never had a bad one. I loved sex. I preferred the partner variety over masturbation, but I hadn't been kidding when I told Mitch it was easier not to get emotionally tangled just to get laid. My right hand worked wonders. But I'd never...I repeat, never...had an orgasm like this one. It gripped me from the inside and pulled me under, holding me in a seemingly endless sea of pure pleasure. Maybe that sounded corny, but it was true as fuck.

I gasped for breath and rode out the inevitable shockwaves before collapsing over my lover. I rolled sideways when Mitch let out an "*Oomph*," wrapping one arm around him so we lay face-to-face. We grinned at each other and then laughed.

"That was fucking amazing. I think I really do love you now," I said.

Mitch snorted in amusement. "I told you so," he singsonged. "The bathroom is around the corner if you want to take that off your junk."

I propped myself on my elbow and looked down at the spent condom on my half-hard dick. "Just give me a coupla tissues. I don't wanna move."

I kneaded his ass gently when he reached for the Kleenex. Then I impulsively molded my chest to his back and pushed my cock against his hole. I didn't intend to enter him, but the tip grazed his entrance and fuck, I wanted to do it all over again. He nudged me away and tossed a few tissues at me.

"Not so fast," he purred.

I slid the condom off, twisting the top as I clandestinely

watched him clean up. He finished up and threw the used tissue and latex into a trash can near the bed before rolling over to face me. I scooted closer and kissed his forehead affectionately.

"That was the best thing I've ever done in my life. And I do mean my entire life," I assured him. I spread my hand over his hip and caressed his ass. "I could do this all night, every night."

He pushed his leg in between mine and smiled. "Me too. Can I ask you something?"

"The answer is yes."

"You don't know what I was going to ask."

I gave him a weak, lopsided smile and shrugged. "Yeah, I do. I did it once before when I was a senior in high school."

"Were you drunk or something?"

"No. It happened naturally over a few months. But the sex—that was a one-time thing. Most of what we did was tame...kissing and grinding. I never saw his dick. He never saw mine. Except maybe in the locker room," I conceded before continuing. "Every time we got together, it was almost like we were surprised by what we were doing. I didn't mean to kiss him but somehow, we'd make out for half an hour in his car in the dark. We'd break apart and look at each other like 'What the fuck?' The next day we wouldn't talk at school or make eye contact on the field, but then we'd do it all over again."

"So he was on your team?"

"Yeah. Graham was our kicker. He transferred in his junior year. He was new in town, new on the team. He was kind of intense, especially about football. I guess I liked that about him. But we weren't friends. We were just horny teenagers trying something new. I didn't know what I was doing and neither did he. We did what felt good. And the one time we actually fucked... it felt *really* good."

"If you liked it, why didn't you do it again?"

"Because afterward...it was a mess. A total fucking awful mess. The last thing I wanted was to do any part of it over again.

Ever. And then you came along." I smoothed his hair back and kissed his forehead. "Thank you."

"For what?"

"Reminding me how good this is."

"It's very very good." He crawled closer still and nudged my shoulder, then laid his head on my chest and wrapped himself around me. "You can stay the night if you want."

"Yeah. I want."

He kissed my cheek and then closed his eyes. I listened to his breathing as I held him. I waited for regret, anxiety, or even claustrophobia to knock me off cloud nine and kill the joy and sense of rightness I felt. But this moment with Mitch was stronger than the past. I felt invincible and in sync with my place in the world in a way I never had before. Something told me he was the key.

6
___

That night changed everything between us. We liked each other. A lot. In a relatively short amount of time, we'd become real friends and now lovers. And in spite of being faux boyfriends for his project, we were a separate entity in private. No one knew about us. Honestly, I kind of liked the element of intrigue. If Derek asked what I was up to, I said I was working on a "project". But truthfully, the project was just an excuse to be with Mitch.

I knew he was being graded on our content, but he didn't talk about it. It would have felt strange to feel as though any part of our conversations were rated or analyzed. Mitch was mine. I didn't want to know if anyone believed we were real. He was real to me. Moreover, he was important to me.

I liked the lilting cadence of his voice, his mischievous smile, and his uncanny attention to detail. He could be serious or silly depending on the situation, but he was always upbeat and fun to be with. And the sex was, quite honestly, the best I'd ever had. Tender kisses quickly escalated to fiery and passionate ones. We pulled at clothing and fumbled with belts and zippers with our mouths fused in an effort to get naked and horizontal as fast as possible.

Mitch was lithe and sure. He moved like a dancer and had the confidence of a gymnast walking a tightrope. But he was sensitive to my inexperience. Or maybe he was gun-shy. Sometimes, I got the impression his breakup with Rory made him cautious. My status as a bi, not quite out of the closet athlete didn't work in my favor. I wanted to change that, though. I wanted him to be as crazy about me as I was for him. And I wanted to spend all my free time with him.

Since he was equally busy, we met after school or practice. If I got out early enough, I'd swing by whatever game he was cheering. But most of the time we did mundane things like meet for coffee or study or cruise the aisles of the local Whole Foods together. We'd walk side by side with our shoulders brushing while we discussed anything from our favorite kinds of cheeses and breakfast cereals to delicacies we wanted to try from other countries.

I fell for him a little more every day. He was so easy to be with, and he laughed at all my dumb jokes. Within a few short weeks, I went from feeling like an explorer in new territory to being part of something much bigger than me. I wasn't alone here. I could tell by the way Mitch looked at me sometimes with pink cheeks and a dreamy expression that he felt it too. Butterflies and all.

We didn't waste time wondering if this was smart. We enjoyed it, so we went for it. All the damn time. At first, I was careful not to spend the night too often. I didn't want to crowd him or ask for more than either of us was ready for, but I couldn't stay away either. When I wasn't with him, I was thinking about what we'd do later. I texted silly questions to be in contact during the day. *What was for dinner? How'd you do on your test? What position do you want to try tonight?* You know, the usual.

What do you know about modern art? I typed before making my way across the grass toward the Humanities building in late October.

The sun filtered through the orange leaves of the amber trees outside in the quad. I loved autumn. Falling leaves, holidays, football season. And Southern California was particularly beautiful this time of year. The days might be shorter, but the mild weather made up for it. My mind wandered to the upcoming weekend just as my phone buzzed in my hand a few seconds later.

A lot. What do you need to know?

I grinned at the screen. *Everything important between 1900 and 1960.*

Mitch responded with a slew of laughing emojis. *That could take all night.*

I guess I better sleep over.

Pjs optional. See you later.

I stuffed my phone into my back pocket and raced up the stairs, pulling the glass door open just as someone called my name. Nicole waved her hands above her head. "Hey, Evan! Just the guy I was hoping to see!"

"Hi, there." I pasted a smile on my face and hooked my thumb behind me. "I gotta run. I'm late to class and—"

"Me too. And mine is two buildings over," she said with a half laugh. She combed a manicured finger through her hair and bit her bottom lip in a move I should have thought was sexy. "I'll be quick. I'm not sure if you know this, but my parents are alumni and they've offered to host a fundraiser after the qualifier game. The invitation is open to everyone on the team, but my dad specifically asked if you could be there."

"Why?"

"He played quarterback and his best friend played your position. His buddy is going to be there too and...it would just be a cool legacy story. I've already asked Christian. He said yes. Think about it and let me know."

Fuck me. I couldn't think of an excuse to miss both without sounding like a dick. I stared at her for a moment then nodded. "Sure. I can stop by."

"Awesome!" She threw her arms around my neck and kissed my cheek before turning for the door.

I stared after her for a second and wondered if I'd been set up. *Nah.* An alumni event was perfectly harmless. I'd been honest a month ago when I told her I wasn't available. And she probably wasn't interested now anyway. It was a school function. Nothing to worry about.

WHEN I MENTIONED Nicole's invitation to Mitch later that night, he gave me a long, hard stare that clearly said, "Boy, someone must have dropped you on your head." Then he went quiet. He propped his book on his knees, turned the page, and resumed studying.

"So you think she's got an ulterior motive?" I asked, plucking his book away and tossing it on the nightstand.

Mitch scowled. "I have no idea, Evan. That's up to you to figure out. Can I have my book, please?"

"No. This is important. Are you mad at me?"

"Of course not. But I'm not going to discuss how you should deal with your admirers. That's up to you."

I sat next to him on the bed and pushed my leg between his open thighs. "She's not a present tense admirer. I told her I'm with you and—"

"No, you told her you were seeing someone. Not the same."

I set my hand on his chin and lightly brushed my thumb across his stubbled jaw. "Baby, look at me. I'm trying to be honest. I don't want to have any secrets."

"But you *are* a secret. You can never really be honest if you have secrets."

"I don't like secrets," I said.

Yeah, it was lame, but I couldn't give him an ETA on coming out. I knew it would happen, but I wanted to do it the right way this time. I couldn't fuck it up and risk losing what I had now.

"Me either. Even when it's no one else's business, something gets screwed up."

"Or someone gets screwed over. Like the time I put gum in my cousin's hair and let my brother take the blame." I made a funny face to lighten the mood.

Mitch rolled his eyes. "That's a different kind of secret."

"Yeah, but he got in trouble for it. I didn't fess up until years later when I was in the hospital and nothing mattered anymore anyway."

"Why were you in the hospital?"

So much for lightening the mood. I was normally pretty good at brushing over that time in my life. A flippant reply about an accident and a quick change of topic worked with most people. Somehow I knew it wouldn't work with Mitch.

"I was in an accident my senior year of high school. It was bad. Broken bones and a punctured spleen."

"Oh. Fuck. I'm sorry."

"Me too. I missed a lot of school, lost a scholarship...but I was lucky. Someone died." I waited a beat, then added, "Graham."

Mitch gasped. "Your boyfriend?"

"No. I told you he wasn't my boyfriend. We just...fooled around. The more we did, the more we wanted to do. But there was so much shame and awkwardness, and it built up every time we were together. He hated himself and then he hated me. And I didn't know how bad it was. If I did, I would have left it alone and saved coming out for college. But I thought I could make a difference if I was honest."

"You *planned* on coming out?"

"Yeah. I was going to do a video," I huffed derisively.

"Like mine."

"Yes, but just one blast to get it out there and be done. *Boom.*

Things were over between Graham and me by then. On one hand, I understood. He was scared. I was too, but I knew my folks would be cool, and I just wanted to be...honest. I was tired of feeling so alone. I didn't buy into the shame the way Graham did. I didn't get how it was possible to feel good with someone one minute and then dirty twenty minutes later. I wanted to know more about who I was, and Graham was my only real frame of reference. So I made a plan.

"I didn't want to blindside him. The problem was, he wouldn't talk to me at school anymore, and he avoided me at practice. I asked one of the guys to drop me off at the park by his house. Graham agreed to meet me and drive me home and... anyway, I told him about my coming-out video. I made it clear it was only about me. I wouldn't name him or mention anything about him, but...he went bonkers. I backed down right away and told him not to worry, 'cause he was shaking and upset. He was driving and I told him to pull over, but he wouldn't and..." I sat up abruptly and swallowed around the bile in my throat. "I really don't know what happened. It was dark. No moon. We were on the freeway. I remember passing the Rose Bowl exit and then...nothing. I woke up in the ICU and...Graham was dead."

Mitch sat up and pulled me into his arms. He held on tightly and didn't ease up until he felt me give in and relax against him. I listened to his heartbeat and smelled the soap on his skin.

When he spoke again, his voice was choked with emotion.

"I'm so sorry, Ev. That's a nightmare."

"Yeah, it was. It was surreal and awful. I was banged up and bruised, but I was still alive. Graham wasn't. I'll never get over that. I remember lying in the hospital bed. The police had just left. They'd asked a million questions about what happened while my mom held my hand. They were trying to make sense of why he'd lost control. And I couldn't tell anyone it was because I wanted to come out."

"Fuck, that's heavy." He wiped a tear from his eye and frowned. "You know it's not your fault."

"I know that now, but at eighteen...let's just say, I was a mess for a while." I let out a humorless half laugh. "I had full-on PTSD. I could hardly process what had happened. I missed months of school. I lost everything. My plans to go to Berkeley for football were gone. I wasn't sure I could go to college at all. And everyone kept saying, 'You're still alive,' like that was so fucking great. Graham was gone, his family was devastated, our team was broken. So, yeah. I felt guilty. And selfish and very fucking confused. You know, his dad used to come see me in the hospital. When he thought I was asleep, he'd talk to me. Pray for me. Tell me God loved me. And I was gonna be all right." I blinked back tears at the memory.

"His parents knew he was gay all along," Mitch said in a hushed tone.

"Yeah, I think so. And mine probably knew it too. But I didn't want to talk about it. I lay there with my eyes closed, thinking if this was what being bi was all about, I didn't want anything to do with it. So much shame and pain and sadness. I figured it was just a matter of controlling myself. If I was bi, so be it. But I was never going to touch a man ever again so there'd never be a reason to tell anyone. My friends didn't need to know. My parents didn't need to know. Fuck coming out." I brushed his hair from his forehead and smiled. "I got pretty good at pushing away anything that had to with that night, including a major part of who I am. I don't feel that way anymore. It took me five years to get here. It feels amazing. So thank you."

Mitch's bottom lip trembled. He threw his arms around my neck and held on tight. "God, I'm glad you're here."

"Me too, baby. Now you know everything about me. Tell me something I don't know about you."

He considered me for a long moment before replying. "I'm afraid of being alone. I don't know what I'll do when my grandmother dies. Her health isn't great and...no one lives forever. When that day comes, I'll really be on my own."

"No, you won't. You'll have me. I'm not going anywhere."

Mitch wiped a tear at the corner of his eye and smiled. "You say you're not romantic, but sometimes you come up with the best lines, Ev."

"Yeah?"

"Yeah."

I brushed my nose against his and kissed him tenderly. I could taste a hint of toothpaste on his breath as I cupped the back of his neck and angled my chin slightly to deepen the connection. He pulled me on top of him, hiking his legs around my waist and holding me close. We made out for a minute or two, lost in soft sighs and tangled limbs. I loved the press of his chest against mine, but my dick throbbed against my zipper. I had to lose some clothing fast. I kneeled between his thighs and pushed my jeans and boxer briefs over my ass, bracing my weight on the headboard to pull the denim off.

"I want to be inside you."

Mitch nodded like a puppet, shoving his workout pants down his legs and whipping his T-shirt off his head before reaching for supplies in the nightstand drawer. I slid a condom on in record time and grabbed the lube from him before he could uncap it.

"What are you doing?"

"I want to try something. Lie back. Please."

I waited for him to obey, then bent over to suck his dick. He'd been on the receiving end of a fair amount of blowjobs recently, so he had to know this wasn't the 'something' I wanted to try. He didn't question me, though. He lifted his hips while I sucked and licked. When I went a little farther south than usual, he propped himself on his elbows to see what I was doing. We held eye contact just as I flattened my tongue and licked his hole.

"Oh, my God. Are you really—"

"Relax and enjoy. I can't do this for long or I'll explode. Just... let me try. Rim job, right?"

Mitch's nostrils flared appreciatively in a lusty acknowledgment of the conversation we had months ago. "Ha. Yeah —oh...wow."

I licked him again and again, teasing the sensitive skin with the tip of my tongue as he writhed beneath me. I sat back abruptly, grabbed the lube and slipped one finger inside him and then another. When he wiggled suggestively, I set my sheathed cock over his entrance and slowly made my way inside him.

We made love for the first time that night. I could say that because I knew for a fact that I'd never done it before in my life. There was meaning behind every sigh and push and pull. We moved with a harmony that reminded me of beautiful lyrics to my favorite songs. Deep kisses, soft moans, and roving hands.

The tempo steadily grew to something more urgent. When he raked his fingers down my back and raised his hips insistently, I took the hint. I drove inside him, thrusting wildly as I bit his lower lip and sucked on his tongue. A tingle of awareness trickled along my spine. I didn't have much time, but I didn't want to go under alone. I went perfectly still for a moment and stared into Mitch's eyes.

"Come now."

And that was all it took.

I roared with the force of my own orgasm as his cum shot between us. We held on to each other until the shaking stopped. Maybe a little longer.

It felt...amazing. Perfect. And as his breathing settled into an even cadence that matched my own, I was overwhelmed by who we were together.

Was this love?

IN ADDITION to our regularly scheduled lives, we were still filming videos for Mitch's project. Our content was funny and original and although Mitch had a decent base of followers, I got the impression most of them were from his LGBTQ clubs and according to the feedback we'd received so far, no one believed we were for real. Chelsea and Derek knew about the project too, but they didn't ask in-depth questions and I, for one, didn't provide details. Truthfully, I rarely saw either of them. And I *lived* with Derek.

We were both in season, so I supposed it made sense, but I got the feeling we were avoiding each other too. I spent the night at Mitch's almost every night. I'd swing by my house after practice, grab something to eat, and wait around till Mitch texted to say he was on his way home. Sometimes I'd leave a dish or cup out to make Derek crazy and remind him he still had a roommate before I headed out again. I thought he might be seeing someone new. When we did bump into each other, I noticed a dreamy look in his eyes that spoke volumes. Or maybe it was the telltale sound of sex in progress coming from his room. Squeaky bed springs and blissed-out moaning. He didn't talk about it, and I didn't ask. I just packed a change of clothes and hightailed it to Mitch's.

Chelsea was different. She was Mitch's best friend, and they weren't the kind of buddies who tiptoed around awkward topics. They talked. They finished each other's sentences and knew secrets no one else did. So while Derek only knew I was working on a "project," Chelsea probably knew everything. I studied their hand motions and the way they walked across the grass with their shoulders brushing. If I hadn't had my dick in his ass eight hours ago, I might have been jealous.

I couldn't decide if it was ironic or just an odd coincidence that Chelsea was besties with the two people I was closest to: Mitch and Derek. Their friendships were totally different. Mitch and Chelsea hung out at parties while Derek and Chelsea were more likely to grab a cup of coffee. But they both adored her and confided in her. He hadn't said so, but I figured Mitch told her about us. And I had to admit, it made me a little nervous to hang out with her.

Chelsea agreed to be our cameraperson for the "sport" segment Mitch wanted to film in the park. The plan was for me to show Mitch how to throw a football and for him to teach me a cheer or a cartwheel or something that hopefully wouldn't require excess exertion. I'd just come from practice and I was exhausted.

I waved as they made their way to me. Chelsea held her arms wide and hugged me before twirling in a circle. She wore a long floral dress with Doc Martens and a wide-brimmed hat that somehow looked very stylish on her. Since we were filming, Mitch had been very specific about our wardrobe. I was instructed to wear dark workout clothes. Preferably black, which he claimed would look fabulous against the autumn foliage. I took a moment to eye his toned physique in his black leggings and matching pullover. Damn, he was sexy.

"Evan, your camera girl is here! Mitchy was just filling me in on his project so far. I've been swamped at work and school and haven't watched a single episode yet, but I'm intrigued. Tell me what you want me to do," she said, flinging her long, dark hair over her shoulder.

"Well, this guy's the boss. Not me. Tell us what the plan is, *Mitchy*." I cupped the back of his neck playfully and ran my fingers through his hair.

He pointed at the football on the picnic table and sighed. "Let's get the hard part over with first. We'll play football, and then we'll do gymnastics. Ready?"

I held up a hand to stop him. "Yeah, but we're not playing football, babe. I'm just going to teach you how to throw a tight spiral."

Chelsea covered her mouth theatrically. "You called him

'babe.' Yes, I can already tell this is going to be good. So what do I do?"

"Um..." Mitch cast a flustered look at me before explaining what he wanted. "Basically, you just follow the action. No jerky movements, though. Keep it as smooth as possible."

"Gotcha. I'll set up the tripod while you two practice your moves. I have one hour, so we should probably concentrate on the action shots now."

"That's fine. We can handle the rest on our own," Mitch said before turning to me. "So how do you throw a spiral...babe?"

I grinned like a madman and tossed the football in the air. "Step right this way. I'll show you how it's done. Grip the ball like so, turn sideways, pull your arm back, and release. But make sure you follow through in one fluid motion. If you don't, the ball will wobble, you'll lose speed, accuracy, and most likely, you'll blow the play."

"Blow the what?" he asked, fluttering his eyelashes flirtatiously.

Chelsea guffawed and held her hand up for a high five. I cast my gaze between them and put my hands on my hips. "All right, then."

"Behave, you two," Mitch chided before turning to me. "I'm going to skip to the outfield, so you can throw your balls to me."

I chuckled and gave Chelsea a funny look but quickly sobered. I shouldn't act so schmoopy in front of her. It was weird.

"Oh, come on, Ev. You know that I know you guys are doing the nasty. Why pretend?" Chelsea huffed.

I twisted the ball in my hands and motioned for Mitch to run farther before turning to her with a serious expression. "I like him. A lot."

"Good. He likes you too."

"Were you surprised?" I asked.

She lowered her giant sunglasses and fixed me with a pointed look. "Shocked. The world is upside down and sideways lately. I don't get it. But he's happy and I like you. Just be good to him, or you'll be dealing with me."

"Got it."

"Good. When are you going to tell Derek?"

I pulled my arm back and fired it across the lawn to Mitch. "Soon. Why?"

"He's your friend, and I'm friends with both of you and—he'll be okay with this, you know. You can trust him."

I adjusted my baseball cap and chuckled at Mitch's antics when the ball hit his fingers and ricocheted off a nearby tree. Then I looked over my shoulder at Chelsea and inclined my head. "I know. We haven't had a chance to talk yet. He's either at school or practice. Or with Gabe. They spend a lot of time together."

"They do, but you should still talk to him. Unless of course, this is a phase and you're more curious than you are actually bi."

"Is that what you think?" I scowled.

"No. I think you're scared. Totally understandable. You're a football player. People will react. Some positive, some negative. And quite a few will be very surprised. But it's your life. You don't own anyone's reaction...just your own. Be happy. And make him happy," she said, gesturing toward Mitch to let me know he was about to throw the ball back.

"Thanks."

Mitch scampered to my side with the ball tucked under his left arm. He gave Chelsea a sign I assumed meant she could start filming before handing the ball to me. "Sorry. That sucked. What am I doing wrong?"

"It didn't suck. That was pretty decent, actually. Let's change it up. I'm gonna run into position, and you can throw it to me. Aim for halfway to that tree," I instructed, pointing to a large oak fifty yards away. "Just watch where I run and let it rip. I'll take it the rest of the way and run this baby into the end zone."

Mitch looked down to fiddle with his grip. When he gave me

a thumbs-up, I ran toward the next tree and turned. I started to retreat when I realized he hadn't released the ball. There was no way he could throw it much farther and—

Suddenly the football whizzed by my head. I shot a wild-eyed look at him before racing after it. I caught it in midstride and kept running...and running. When I reached the huge oak, I spiked the ball the raised my arms victoriously. Then I ran back to Mitch, picked him up, and tackled him onto the grass.

"*Oomph.* You're crushing me."

I braced myself over him and grinned. "You're cute and I really wanna kiss you right now."

"Chelsea's filming," he warned with a mischievous grin that doubled as a dare.

I never could resist a dare.

I sealed my mouth over his in a passionate kiss before jumping up and yanking him to his feet. I broke into a mini touchdown dance that made him laugh and fuck, I suddenly felt like I was floating on air. Something in me screamed that this was how it was supposed to be. I could have this forever if I was brave.

Chelsea was mostly quiet while she filmed, but she cheered when Mitch caught the ball and chortled merrily at my lame-ass cheering skills and even worse cartwheel. Mitch thanked her profusely. Then he pushed Pause and gave her a thorough once-over. She did the same to him. The silent standoff was slightly unsettling. I was relieved when Chelsea finally turned to hug me.

"I love this. There's a huge audience out there you haven't tapped into. Can I share your link on social media?" she asked.

Mitch frowned. "I don't know. I—"

"The more data you collect, the better. I'm totally okay with it," I intercepted. "Why not spread the word?"

"Chels's audience is more varied and far-reaching than mine. I've purposely limited my exposure. I changed my handle and only invited people from my class and the LGBTQ Center and—"

"Why would you do that? I thought the idea was to get more viewers to collect data. This is for a grade, right?"

"I think this is where I scoot. Let me know what you want to do." Chelsea kissed Mitch's cheek and hugged me again before leaving us.

"Well?" I prodded. "What am I missing? I thought you had more followers than her."

Mitch perched on the corner of the bench. "Under my own name, that's true. But I made a new account for this project. I might have fifty viewers. It's not ideal, but I'll get a decent grade and—"

"Why would you keep it a secret?"

I watched his Adam's apple move in his throat. He shifted on the bench and then shrugged. "I thought you might change your mind in the beginning. I didn't want to introduce us to everyone and end up embarrassed when you pulled out. We have too much overlap. It would have been awkward. But when you didn't go anywhere, I didn't want to share you. I didn't want anyone to point out all the reasons we'd never work. I didn't want anyone to tell me what I already know. You're good-looking, athletic, popular....You're out of my league."

"That's not true."

"It's perception. And that's what the project is about. A few people giving their two cents is normal. Thousands...I don't know if I'm ready to lose quite so publicly."

"Lose what?"

"You," he replied quietly.

I sat beside him and pulled him against my side. "You aren't going to lose me."

"Evan, the only reason this works is because no one knows about us. And before you say it, my grandmother and best friend don't count. In my experience, when more than five people know a closeted person is in a gay relationship, it's just a matter of time before it all goes to shit."

"I'm not Rory, and I—"

"But the story is the same!" He sighed in frustration and pulled away from me. "I'm a fucking magnet for gorgeous men with secret bi sides. It's not you. It's me."

"Well, I think that's bullshit. You've already decided you know I'm gonna fail. You haven't given me a chance. I want a fair shot. Tell Chelsea to promote your page and then cross promote on your real site. Do this right and let's get the fuckin' A," I insisted.

"But—"

"No 'buts.' Don't tell me I'm gonna lose."

"This isn't a game."

"I know what it is, and I know how I feel about you. Trust me."

He met my gaze with a challenging one. "It's a big audience, Ev."

"How big?"

"A few hundred thousand."

Oh. Wow. Way bigger than I thought.

"Do it."

"You're sure?"

"Positive."

Mitch's smile was more tentative than happy. It lacked confidence and though I wanted to be insulted, I understood. He was used to being left behind. By selfish parents and ex-boyfriends who put their insecurities before him. Geez, his last relationship was with a guy who tried to win him back by making him jealous...with a girl. He hadn't had anyone go out on a limb and tell the whole fucking world how incredible he was. It wasn't right. But I could change that.

7

Derek's car was parked in the driveway later that night. That didn't necessarily mean he was home. He spent a lot of time with Gabe, and I'd noticed they used his teammate's car, which might have been to throw me off guard. Maybe that sounded paranoid, but I had a feeling the reason we didn't see each other as often had more to do with his relentlessly squeaky bedsprings than a busy schedule.

Just last week, I'd left Mitch's bed before dawn, driven home on empty city streets, tiptoed into my house and down the hall toward the bedrooms, only to stop short at the telltale sounds of sex coming from Derek's room. The masculine grunts were reminiscent of what Mitch and I had been doing a few hours earlier. As long as I'd known Derek, he'd only been with women, but the walls were too thin to mask the obvious. So we were both bi. I'd heard their grand finale, punctuated with a loud moan and then soft laughter, and wondered if I should tell him I knew. And tell him about me.

I didn't tell him that day, but I promised myself I would soon. When I was ready.

Maybe today.

I changed my clothes after practice that afternoon and was about to head to the kitchen when the door next to me clicked open. I listened to footsteps move down the hall, hushed whispers, and then the front door opening and closing. When I thought the coast was clear, I tiptoed down the hall to the kitchen.

Derek walked in a few minutes later with serious bedhead and a sappy looking smile that faded slightly when he saw me.

"Oh. Hi. I didn't know you were home. Don't you have practice?" he asked.

"Done for the day. I got home fifteen minutes ago."

"Oh." His face went bright red.

I held up a cup just as he was about to turn around. "Want water?"

"Uh...yeah. Thanks." He licked his lips nervously and leaned against the counter. "I heard about that YouTube thing you're doing with Mitch. Is that the secret project you've been talking about?"

I gave myself a mental pep talk as I handed him a water bottle. Derek was cool, and apparently he was going through the same thing as me. I could do this now.

"Yeah," I grunted. *Lame.*

"How's it going? I haven't watched any of it, but Chels said you guys look like a very convincing couple."

"It's going well. Um...how's Gabe?"

"Gabe? He's fine. Why?"

I shrugged. "No reason. Want to play Mortal Kombat? We're up to part five. We gotta keep going."

"Yeah, sure."

We exchanged guarded smiles, then headed for the living room. So much for coming out.

THERE WAS a huge difference between fifty followers and three hundred and fifty thousand. Who knew? I had to be one of the last holdouts when it came to social media immersion. I checked a couple of sites once a day and looked at pictures my friends tagged me in. And the only YouTube videos I'd watched had something to do with football or extreme sports, featuring daredevil maneuvers even I wouldn't attempt. I didn't post much myself, so it didn't occur to me to think about who was virtually engaged in my everyday life. Until now.

The buzz grew daily. My meager following exploded overnight. Strangers from all over the world commented on GIFs and photos I'd posted months ago and asked invasive and sometimes inappropriate questions about my relationship with Mitch. How often did we have sex? Did I like giving or receiving blowjobs? Who topped whom? You know, the usual. When a cousin in Italy asked my dad if I was gay, I knew it was a matter of time before one of my teammates or friends asked what the hell I was doing. And because everything happens at the speed of light on the internet, I didn't have to wait long.

Jonesie cornered me in the locker room after practice the following week.

"What's with that YouTube thing? I heard you're playing gay for a real gay dude's online TV pilot."

"TV pilot?" I repeated with an eye roll. This was how rumors got started.

"Yeah. My sister said some of those social media dorks make big bucks in advertising. It's a clever idea, but I don't know about the gay stuff. Does your girlfriend know?" he asked, pulling his T-shirt over his head.

"I don't have a girlfriend, Jonesie."

He frowned. "I thought things were getting heavy with you and Nicole."

"You thought wrong. As far as the YouTube stuff goes...you're supposed to subscribe to his channel and vote. Is it real? Yes or no?"

"I vote no."

"Why?"

" 'Cause I've seen you with Nicole."

"What the fuck are you talking about? I haven't seen her since—"

"Yesterday at Christian's barbeque," he intercepted. "She was all over you, and you fuckin' loved it."

Only part of that statement was true. I'd promised Christian I'd swing by his place for an end of season pool party. I'd stayed for a beer and a burger and spent most of the time swapping stories with my teammates. Nicole had been there, and yeah, she was a little handsy and clingy. I'd been friendly but not overly so. I took a few selfies with her and some friends and got the fuck out.

"Wrong again, Jonesie."

"She said you're going with her to that fund raiser Saturday."

"I said I'd go. I didn't say I'd go *with* her," I corrected.

"Hmph. Playin' it cool. I get it. Whatever. You're one of us. You play football. You're not queer, dude." He made the universal "yuck" face, then hollered across the room. "Hey, what do you guys think? Is di Angelo a fruitcake? Raise your hand if you vote yes."

The room broke out into a mostly good-natured debate about my sexuality. I was torn between being irate at the personal invasion to sweating bullets. I could come clean here and now. I knew locker room etiquette better than most of these idiots. Taking offense was the worst thing I could do. I had to put together a decent speech, but my brain wasn't working. And I wasn't good at talking about my feelings on the best days. Christian was better at this stuff than me, I mused, glancing over at our quarterback.

Christian met my gaze, then looked away. I couldn't read him, but he didn't look happy. He was either offended on my behalf or pissed that we'd devolved to sophomoric levels of idiocy. Yes, I had an opportunity to speak out, but this atmosphere was too much like the one I remembered in high school. And something in Christian's eyes reminded me of Graham.

My mind was suddenly on fire. *Say something. Do something. Be brave. Act now.*

But I couldn't. I was paralyzed by fear. And every second that passed with questioning glances and uncomfortable laughter weighed on me heavily. I had to do something or I'd pass out.

So I threw my towel at Jonesie's head and chuckled when he draped it over his ears like a scarf. "I just farted on that. You're welcome," I said with a wink.

He whipped the towel off and snapped it at my ass and as a new round of silliness broke over the room, I felt myself inch closer to an invisible edge. Any moment now, I'd lose my footing and everything around me would change. I had to be ready for it.

THE NEXT FEW days were weird as hell. I went to practice but skipped a couple of classes to minimize my time on campus. I felt exposed in a way I didn't like. Maybe it was my imagination, but I sensed stares and whispers reminiscent of my high school days after the accident. I downplayed the sudden interest when Mitch asked if I'd noticed anything new. I claimed everything was the same, and maybe it was. Maybe I was different. Not stronger, braver, or smarter, though. Just...different. I felt like I was stuck on a fourth down, inches from the goal line, waiting for the coach to call the play that would drive me into the end zone. It was becoming clear that I couldn't rely on instruction. The move was mine to make, I mused as I pulled into a parking space near the gymnasium.

On a whim, I'd decided to catch the last half of the volleyball game Mitch was cheering and watch him in action. I'd made excellent time on the drive from our team dinner, and I wasn't ready to go home yet. The busier I stayed, the better. When my schedule slowed, I had more time to think and at the moment, that was kind of dangerous.

The attendant checking IDs and collecting money from non-students at the door waved me in free of charge and instructed me to sit wherever I wanted. The later hour and under-capacity crowd probably saved me five bucks. I sat three rows back on the home bleachers and searched the floor for Mitch.

My heart flipped against my rib cage when I spotted him on the sidelines in his black-and-gold cheer squad uniform. He stood tall and proud, with his chin tilted toward the rafters as though he were performing to a sellout crowd instead of a few parents and friends. I felt a surge of awe and adoration for him. And gratitude that he was mine.

I leaned forward with my elbows on my knees just as a perky blonde with freckles sat beside me.

She bounced excitedly and widened her eyes. "Oh, my gosh. I've totally been watching your IG and YouTube channel. You and Mitch are the cutest! Please tell me you're real! You must be. You wouldn't come to one of these games unless you were a couple. You don't even go to school here, right?"

"Uh...no, but—"

"Can I get a selfie with you?"

"Well, um...okay."

She put her arm around me and snapped a photo before I had a chance to smile. "Would you be willing to do another one with my friends? It'll only take a sec," she pleaded.

I complied. She was a fast picture-taker and other than causing a mini-sensation in a half-empty gym, I honestly didn't see the harm in appeasing a gaggle of freshman girls. This was becoming a regular thing. I'd been stopped a few times this week alone by random people who wanted me to know they thought our videos were funny and entertaining.

The bubbly girl took the photo, then hollered Mitch's name, announcing my presence to my mystified-looking lover before returning to her seat with her friends. Mitch smiled at me and got back to work, revving up the meager crowd from the sidelines. He was good at this. His enthusiasm was contagious but a little lost on a small audience.

I glanced around the gym again then did a double take when I noticed someone filming me from the opposite side of the court. A young woman with long brown hair turned her phone to Mitch and then back to me shamelessly. She clearly didn't care that I knew she was watching me. In fact, she probably liked it. I might understand if I was famous. But I wasn't. I was just me. Maybe it was a good thing Mitch hadn't used his real name until recently. The near constant attention and prying eyes freaked me out.

I pulled my cell out and lowered my head to avoid unwanted scrutiny as I scrolled through missed messages. The first was from Nicole.

There's a cocktail party on campus before the fundraiser Saturday. Can't wait to see you!

I'd ignored an earlier message from Jonesie giving me the same info and basically begging me to be there. I pulled up his text as I glanced at the volleyball sailing over the net and typed a quick reply.

I can't wait.

The sarcasm would probably be wasted on him, but Jonesie was always going to see what he wanted. I was about to slip my phone into my jacket pocket when a flurry of hearts lit the screen. *What the fuck?*

Nicole's message thread popped up. She must have added to her text just as I thought I was replying to Jonesie.

The event will run late. You can spend the night, she'd written.

And my reply...*I can't wait.*

Fuck.

I studied the message and tried to think of a nice way to say

"Just kidding," or "That was a mistake." But the buzzer went off, signaling the end of the game and suddenly clarifying my intentions didn't seem important. I didn't owe Nicole or Jonesie or anyone else an explanation. It wasn't their business.

I glanced up at the stranger recording me across the way and froze at the sickening realization that I'd let them in. I was completely exposed, like a bug under a microscope or a caged animal. People were waiting for me to reveal myself. They wanted to be assured that I hadn't changed and if I had, they wanted to know how and why. They wanted to know what my choices said about them. Maybe we all needed validation, justification, or a cause to stand behind, a reason to love or a reason to hate.

But this was mine. No one else's.

I licked my lips nervously and searched for Mitch. I had to get out of here. Being with him was all that mattered.

WE WERE all over each other when we walked into my place that night. Derek was at a tournament, and I didn't want to pass up spreading out in a bigger accommodation, even if it was just for a few hours. I waited for Mitch to park his car and join me on the porch before closing the door, pushing his jacket off his shoulders, and his shirt over his head. We stumbled down the hallway, tearing clothes off with our mouths fused and our hands everywhere. I couldn't be bothered to fully remove my clothes. Getting inside him was the main objective. The rest would happen in good time.

I shoved my jeans around my knees and held his hips, thrusting my bare cock against his crack while he unwrapped a condom. Mitch turned around and fell to his knees to suck me until I yanked at his hair and pumped my hips in a telltale rhythm that meant I wasn't going to last. Then he slipped the latex on me, crawled to the middle of my bed, and swayed his ass from side to side. He sucked in a sharp breath when I entered him. I went as still as possible, massaging his sides before slowly making my way inside my lover.

Mitch groaned and pushed back insistently. "Harder. Do it harder. And say that thing you say sometimes."

I drove into him and flattened myself over his smaller body. "What do I say?"

"My hole. Tell me what you want to do to me. Fuck me."

My mouth went dry. *Holy shit.* I slipped my hand underneath him, stroking him while I licked his ear and whispered a litany of naughty things I wanted to do to him while I thrust my hips, driving into him as he clutched at the sheets with white knuckles. I rained kisses on his nape and shoulders, jacking his cock in a frenzy. I wanted release; at the same time, I never wanted this to end. And when my orgasm hit, I came so hard I couldn't stop shaking until Mitch fell apart a moment later.

WE CLEANED UP, redressed, and made our way to the kitchen. I paused with my hand on the refrigerator door and looked over at Mitch. His sex-mussed hair and wrinkled uniform shirt did things to me. Or maybe it was his lopsided smile. God, I had it bad for him. This was what mattered. Us. No one else was welcome here.

"Want something to eat?"

"No, thanks. Is Derek coming home?"

"I don't know. He might be with Gabe."

"So did he finally tell you?"

I grabbed a container of leftover pasta and nodded. "Yeah. How did you know?"

"Chelsea."

"Right." I pulled a fork from the drawer and leaned against the counter. "He was having a bad day and...it all came out. Actually, I had to prod him a bit, but it turns out my roommate has a boyfriend."

"Did you tell him about me?" he asked with faux nonchalance.

"No. It wasn't really a good time." And I wasn't ready. I kept that part to myself and shoveled in a bite of spaghetti to keep myself from saying it aloud.

"Oh."

"Your fan club showed up in full force tonight," I commented around a mouthful of food.

"The freshman girls?" He chuckled as he uncapped a water bottle. "Yeah. They're sweet. They've followed me for a while, but they've gone bonkers since I published the links to our videos."

"Hmm. I've got a lot of new followers suddenly too. And people looking at me funny at school. I think I should come out on your video," I blurted, out of the fucking blue.

"Excuse me?"

"You heard me. We can do it together."

"No. I don't think that's a good idea."

I stared at him for a second in surprise. In light of my freak-out at the gym, I thought it was fucking brilliant. If he was with me, I could do anything. "Why not? We talked about this. We both want this."

"You have to come out on your own. Not with me. I'm already out, and I have my own story. This one is all you. It's too personal a statement to attach to someone else's school project. It's got to be yours, and it has to be real."

"It *is* real," I insisted. "Why not get it out there all at once? It's a good idea."

"It's okay. But the videos aren't real, Evan. They're scripted. Sure, we ad-lib and we both know there's truth under the silly questions about sex and intense debates about Grandma's cookies, but you have other parts of your life that are partially scripted too. The way you act with your football friends and that girl who thinks she still has a shot with you."

"Nicole?"

"If you say so," he retorted.

I furrowed my brow. "She wouldn't think so if I came out."

"Sure she would. She's been busy posting photos from parties and football games lately. Did you know that? She posted something an hour ago...a text thread about your date on Saturday."

I gaped at him in surprise. "Are you kidding me? That just happened, and it's not even true."

Mitch gave me a sharp look. "It doesn't matter. It's out there."

"I agreed to go to the fund raiser, but it's not a date. I'm not going with *her*. I'm just attending. The text messages got scrambled with one I was sending Jonesie and—come on, Mitch. You know I'm not interested in Nicole."

"Yeah, I know. But it's kind of fuzzy to everyone else. So coming out on a video you're doing with me is just white noise. It's a titillating sound byte that may or may not be sincere. Get it? 'Faux or No?' It's just another plot twist. Viewers will eat it up."

"So? Isn't that a good thing?"

"I don't think so." He sighed unhappily and looked away. "It makes me feel a little sick."

"Will you feel better if I come out?"

He frowned and bit his bottom lip hard. I wasn't sure what he was thinking, but I was obviously saying all the wrong things. I felt like I was moving in the dark, bumping into furniture, and waking up old ghosts.

"You've asked me that so many times, Ev. My answer is never going to change. *If* you come out, it has to be your idea. Not mine."

"I didn't mean 'if,' I meant 'when,' " I explained, putting my fork in the container and setting it on the counter. "Look, I thought you'd be cool with this."

"Cool with what? Being real fake boyfriends? No. I'm not cool with it. I never wanted to be fake anything. This wasn't supposed to happen," he said, clearly agitated.

"Hey, we aren't fake. We're real. You know we are. Everyone else is weighing in now too. They're taking pictures and videos and following us around and...why not tell them the truth? I thought we were on the same page here. I thought you wanted...us."

"I do. I want us. I want you. I'm so in lo—I want too much."

Tears trickled down his cheeks. He swiped them away with the back of his hand and looked away. I moved into his space and held him close. "Why are you crying?"

"This isn't gonna work. Not now. You need space."

I let him go and lifted his chin. "No, I don't. It's working. It's good. We're good."

"No. Don't you get it? You can't come out because of me. Or anyone else. I keep saying, 'When you're ready,' but you can't be ready if you're being smothered by thousands of strangers who want to know your shoe size one minute and who you really fuck the next. You have a real life with family and friends who love you. You don't need the strangers."

"But I need you," I said softly.

"You have me. I'm not going anywhere. I'm just making room for you."

My brow creased so hard I had a headache. "Is that code for something? I'm not good at codes. What are you saying?"

"I can't be in your way."

"That's still code. You're not in the way. We're doing a project together," I said lamely.

"I'll turn it in as is."

"And then what?"

"It's over." His voice cracked, and tears pooled in his eyes.

My brain fought hard to make sense of the wild turn of events. I'd been inside him fifteen minutes ago. Now he wanted out?

"Why? You don't want that. I don't want that. Why?"

"Because I'm always the one who clings a little too hard and asks a little too much, and I'm not going to do it this time. When you tell the world who you are, there should be no guilt, no sorrow, no shame. And there shouldn't be a guy on the side with a camera and a microphone hoping thousands of viewers will vote for us. You have to want it for yourself."

I pursed my lips and swallowed hard. "I do."

"We're at different places, Evan. I can't pretend anymore. I told you that I kept the project small on purpose. If you'd been anyone else, I wouldn't have bothered, but I liked you too much right from the start. So I decided to wait for you to tell me you wanted out. But you didn't. And every day this thing inside me has grown. It didn't happen out of the blue. It was little by little. The way you put pink licorice in my pockets and leave your shoes on my floor. The twenty silly texts you send me when you're bored in class. The way you stop to talk to my grandmother no matter how big of hurry you're in. You're the best person I know, Ev. And it's a big problem for me because I don't just like you now. I love you."

I opened my mouth in shock. "You love...Then stay."

"I can't. You have to be free to think without me in the way. No regrets." He pushed his hands through his hair and stepped away. "I should go and—"

"Please don't," I whispered. "Please. I'm trying not to mess up, and I'm doing it anyway. But just—give me a chance."

Mitch pulled me against him and buried his face in my neck. His tears wet the collar of my T-shirt and once again, I was at a loss. I wanted to console him, but my heart felt oddly fragile, like it was cracking into pieces faster than I could put them back together. I held on for as long as he let me. But when he kissed my cheek and pushed away, I had no choice. I let go.

WHEN I WOKE up in the ICU five years ago with a bunch of broken bones and a seriously fucked up future, I hadn't thought anything worse could happen. Then they told me Graham died in the crash. And the real clincher—it appeared he wanted to end his life that night. It took me much longer to recover from the mental anguish than the broken bones. If there'd been a way to trade the cloak of darkness that pulled me under for months after for another round of shattered limbs, I'd have taken that option any day.

After years of therapy, I finally turned a corner. I was in a good place. I had a supportive family, great friends, and in a few months, I'd be a college graduate. But I'd never felt worse. And given my past, that was saying something.

I walked around in a daze for twenty-four hours after Mitch left, going through the motions and trying to figure out what I was supposed to do next. It was my move, right? I was on my own. If I wanted to make my own video, I could. If I wanted to make a few phone calls instead, that was okay too. Or I could forget the whole thing and go back to the way I was before Mitch came along.

No. I couldn't. I wasn't the same person. I couldn't pretend I wasn't broken all over again. The difference was, I could fix it myself if I was brave.

By day two, I began to suspect I'd left all my bravado on the field. I felt weak and unsure, and so unbelievably sad that it hurt to move. I lay on the sofa with a bag of potato chips on my stomach, watching sports highlights on mute. I had no idea what time it was, but it had to be closing in on midnight. I should sleep or something, I mused as the front door clicked open.

Low masculine voices broke the silence. *Fuck.* It would take more energy than I had to turn off the television and fake sleep. It wouldn't work anyway. Derek had a thing about crumbs. He'd wake me up just to get the potato chips out of my hands. I sat up and set the bag on the coffee table just as Derek and Gabe walked into the room.

"Hi. I thought you'd be out...or asleep," Derek said.

"I'm going to bed now."

I shared a knowing glance with Gabe when Derek reached for the bag of potato chips, folding the seam precisely. No doubt he'd caught on right away that his boyfriend was a world-class neat freak.

"Good. It's two a.m. Don't you have a game tomorrow?"

"Yeah, Mom. I do. I think." I sat up gingerly and rubbed the back of my neck before attempting to stand.

"Are you sick?" Derek gave me a suspicious once-over.

"I'm fine. Just tired."

Gabe flopped into the chair next to me and picked up the remote. He didn't change the channel or adjust the sound, though. He sat quietly and waited for us to finish up our middle of the night pleasantries. I could end it by going to bed, but I didn't have the energy to move yet.

"What happened?" Derek asked softly.

"Nothing happened," I lied.

"Then why aren't you with Mitch?"

I felt my defenses rise around me like an invisible brick wall. I looked up at Derek and prepared a scornful speech letting him know he had the wrong idea about me. But the second I opened my mouth, the wall began to slowly crumble. I couldn't lie to my newly un-closeted friend and his boyfriend. I'd been too engrossed in my own drama to pay close attention, but I knew they'd gone through a lot just to be together. Not as teammates. As lovers. Pleading ignorance at this point would be insulting and dishonest. Derek deserved better than that.

"He told me I needed space. Or maybe he needed space. And since he's not returning my texts and calls, I think that means... you know." I couldn't even say it. My chest was heavy. It hurt to breathe. It hurt to talk.

"Oh." Derek sat on the coffee table, bracing his elbows on his knees. "What are you going to do?"

I sighed heavily and shrugged. "I don't know. He took his project down. Erased everything. Some of it was really good too."

"It was great. Even if you weren't a couple, you guys had chemistry," Gabe commented.

"We *were* a couple," I said without thinking. "It was real."

An uncomfortable silence settled over the room. I braved a glance at Derek, who simply nodded. "I know."

"You know? How did you know?" I whispered in awe. "When?"

"Recently." He looked at Gabe then back at me. "I think we've been going through this at the same time. I didn't know you were..."

"Bi." *There. I said it.* The word sounded funny coming from me and referring to me, but Gabe and Derek didn't seem to notice.

"Yes. Bi." He smiled wanly then continued, "You spent a lot of time with Mitch but I didn't know anything until I saw a video. The way you looked at him sort of gave you away. But I was still too caught up with Gabe and school and polo, and I didn't want to say anything. I figured you'd tell me when you were ready. If you're not ready, that's cool. I'm around if you want to talk."

Tears stung my eyes. I didn't trust my voice, but I managed a brief, "Thanks."

"I just want to remind you that you told me I should be true to myself and love who I wanted. It's good advice. And I know it's always easier to give advice than take it yourself but...dude, you only get one life. One chance. Be good to yourself. You're stronger than you know."

"You sound like you're reading cocktail napkins at a yoga wine and cheese party," I huffed with a half laugh as I clandestinely wiped at my eyes.

Gabe leaned forward and kissed Derek's temple and chuckled. "He's right, though. Do what makes you happy. The rest is bullshit."

I nodded in agreement. It was all bullshit.

Yet somewhere under the lies of omission, posturing, and flat-out denial, there was truth. Telling it would take a fuckload of courage, but I didn't have a chance if I didn't go for it. And doing nothing at all was another form of giving up. Not okay.

8

My brain buzzed all night with Olympic-caliber inspirational ideas to win my man back. I was Rocky Balboa training on the stairs in Philadelphia, Babe Ruth hitting his longest home run, and the whole USA hockey team winning a miracle on ice. Blood pulsed through my veins to an internal soundtrack encouraging me to give everything I had to come up with the ultimate win. But nothing was going to happen if I didn't make a few key moves first.

First, I sent a text to Mitch asking him to come to my game. He wasn't responding to my messages so I sent a backup one to Chelsea asking for help. Of course she didn't just say yes.

Why? What if he says no? she asked.

Tell him it's important.

And if he still says no?

Please, Chelsea. I'll owe you for life. I stared at the message helplessly and added one more pathetic *Please*.

Next, I texted Nicole.

Thanks for the invite to the fund raiser, but I won't be able to make it.

It was short and direct, and given the circumstances, it was all

I needed to say. I barely knew the girl, and I had no interest in playing cyber games with selfies and misleading messages. I sucked at mind games and innuendo anyway. If it wasn't real, I wasn't interested.

And then, I called home.

I didn't think this part would be too hard. My parents didn't care if I wasn't the smartest, strongest, or bravest. They accepted me as I was, and they'd always made an effort to be there for my brother and me. When my life had literally been in the balance, they'd made sure I knew I had their love and support. No matter what.

Unfortunately, that didn't make me less anxious. I swiped my damp palms on my jeans and ran through the speech I'd prepared in my head one last time before pushing Send.

Mom picked up on the first ring. "Oh! Look at you! Are we really FaceTiming? This is fun!"

I let out a half laugh and leaned against my headboard. "Yeah. Real fun. Um…is Dad home too?"

"He's right here." She swiveled her phone and instructed my father to say hello.

He pulled his reading glasses off and set his iPad aside before greeting me. "You're still in bed?" he teased. "Must be nice."

"No. I've been up for hours," I assured him with a wan smile. It felt like days.

"Oh. Did you have practice?"

"Not yet. Um…you're coming tonight, right?"

"Of course! It's a big game. We wouldn't miss it," Dad said enthusiastically.

Mom nudged his shoulder and adjusted the screen so she was mostly in the frame. Then she narrowed her eyes and gave me one of her patented no-nonsense looks. The one she used to remind me she was an expert at sniffing out trouble.

"What's wrong, Evan?" Mom asked.

"Nothing," I lied. "But I have to tell you something and…"

"What is it?" she prodded when I stalled. "Are you okay? You look fine. Are you sick? Did you get hurt? Is it your knee?"

"Mom, I'm okay. Really. I'm healthy. That's not it."

I pushed my free hand through my hair and fixated on the football on my desk before refocusing on my parents' worried expressions. Fuck, I shouldn't have FaceTimed. But I couldn't wait till later and risk them hearing my news from someone else. And there wasn't enough time to drive to Pasadena and back before I had to be at the field. This was it.

"Don't make me guess, Evan. I can feel my hair turning gray. Could you please just—"

"I'm gay," I blurted. I shook my head and released a rush of air before continuing in a fast clip, as though I had seconds to get the words out and make them count. "Actually, I'm bi. And I think you already know and I don't think you care but if you do...well, I can't change it. I can't deny it anymore either."

"O...kay," Mom replied cautiously.

She didn't seem less worried, so I kept talking, turning my gaze back to the football, like a focal point in a spinning room. "I figured I should tell you myself, so you know it's real and not some internet rumor. I should have said it a long time ago, but...I didn't want to be this way."

"Oh Evan," she said in a pained tone.

"It's true. I swore after Graham...after everything that happened...I wasn't gonna talk about it. It's really hard to say out loud and it's hard to explain why I feel the way I do. I'm not ashamed. I'm cool with who I am as a person, but for the first time I feel like I'm on the outside. It's different. But I'm *not* different. I'm still me. And I...I didn't want you to think I've changed, you know? 'Cause I haven't." I swallowed hard and repeated. "I'm just...me."

I glanced at my screen when my mom's breath hitched audibly. She dabbed at the corner of her eyes and leaned against Dad's shoulder.

"Oh, Evan, we know," she said. "We love you exactly the way you are."

I gulped around the grapefruit lodged in my throat and nodded. "I love you too."

"You must have met someone. Is it the young man from the videos? When can we meet him?" she asked softly.

I wiped a tear off my cheek and barked a quick laugh that had more to do with a sense of relief than humor. "Soon. I hope. I—thank you."

"Don't thank us," Dad interjected in a heavier than usual accent. "*Noi ti amiamo figlio*. We know who you are and we know how strong you are...in your spirit. That is where strength counts."

I nodded, too choked up to reply. Mom touched her screen and flashed a teary smile. "We've seen you suffer, Ev. We've seen you fall down and pick yourself up and start over again. We've seen you conquer your fears like a true champion. We are in awe of you, baby. We stand by you. We respect you and we are honored to be your parents. We love you. To the next galaxy and back."

I sniffed loudly and rubbed my nose in a valiant attempt to get my emotions under control.

"So...tell us about him. What's he like?" Dad asked.

"He's awesome. His name is Mitch. You're gonna like him. Of course, I gotta make him like *me* again, but—"

"You will," Mom assured me.

"Yeah. I will."

A FEW HOURS LATER, I wasn't sure how anything was going to play out. From the moment I'd stepped into the locker room, I'd felt like I was moving in slow motion. My concentration was shot and my nerves were on edge. I adjusted my shoulder pads and leaned in to check for any incoming messages. I hadn't heard back from Chelsea since noon when she promised to try. Try. *Ugh.* That word frustrated me. I was hoping for a "Don't worry, Ev. You've got this." Or better yet, a "Mitch still loves you. Stop freaking out."

Did I love him? Yeah, I did. The feeling wasn't what I'd expected, though. I thought love would be sweet and dreamy, like the world's best and longest-lasting orgasm. In reality, it was more like a heart-thumping roller coaster ride with hair-raising twists that turned you inside out. But it was more life-affirming than anything I'd ever experienced. I had to win him back. I took a deep breath and let the noise filtering through the open locker room door take over.

The stadium seemed louder than ever. I supposed it made sense. This was an important playoff game. Whoever won would head on to the championship. Nerves were high, and adrenaline levels were through the roof. Division Three teams might not garner the notoriety some of the more elite programs did, but we had an impressive base of supporters who'd turned up in throngs tonight to cheer us on. The lights, noise, and feverish quality in the mid-November air were reminiscent of a rock concert. Our fans came to see us kick ass, and we were going to do our best to deliver.

Christian called us into a huddle for one of his usual pregame speeches. I grabbed my helmet and was about to close my locker when my cell vibrated. My heart slammed against my chest when I picked it up...and then took a nosedive. It wasn't Chelsea. It was Nicole.

Please come, Evan. It's an important event for the school. Just a quick date.

Thank you, but I can't. I swallowed hard and glanced around the bustling locker room at the fierce-looking jocks head-butting, pushing, shoving, and riling each other up to kick some ass out on the field. Then I glanced at my screen and added, *My boyfriend wouldn't approve.*

My finger hovered over the button for half a second, and then I pressed Send. My heart raced like I'd run a marathon but fuck, it felt good too. It would feel better when I knew I actually had a boyfriend, but I'd fix that part later. I tossed my phone inside my bag, closed my locker, and hurried to join my teammates.

"...we got this," Christian was saying. "We're better, we're faster, we're stronger, and this is our house. No one is gonna beat us here. Am I right?" He waited for our explosive whoops to die down before continuing. "Those are our people. Our fans."

"Mostly Evan's though," Jonesie piped in.

"Shut up, Jones," Christian snapped. "Now let's do this. One, two, three..."

I cheered along with the rest of the guys, then stepped back to adjust the strap on my helmet. I waited for Jonesie to do the same before I popped him upside the head. "What was that crack for?"

"Your YouTube fans are out there with rainbow flags and posters that say, 'Evan and Mitch Forever.' You better make us look good out there, or everyone is gonna think you're a fag, dude," he huffed.

"Ignore him. Let's go." Christian smacked my ass on his way out the door.

"No. Stop!"

I waited for Christian to turn around. The rest of the guys grumbled like bulls at the starting gate, but I knew they'd take Christian's lead. He had a commanding presence that resonated on our team. They liked my good-natured bluster. I could incite a riot with a goofy chant and get the troops revved up for battle, but when Christian spoke, they stopped to listen.

"What is it?"

"My timing is weird but...if there really are signs out there—"

"We'll ignore them. Don't worry about it," Christian assured me.

"You don't have to ignore them. It's true. I'm bi." I pulled my helmet off and kept my eyes on the exit sign above the door.

I was the antithesis of cool. My timing wasn't just weird. It was fucked up. I'd made an already intense pregame situation fifty shades of awkward by making it about me. Everyone who'd ever played a sport knew there was no "I" in "team." But I couldn't keep it inside anymore. This had been bottled tight for five years. It had been seeping out of me in fits and starts since Chelsea's party months ago and now...I was out.

"Okay. All right. That's cool," Christian said. He held my gaze for a long moment and then turned to look around at the flurry of confused faces partially hidden in black helmets. "Anybody got anything to say, or are we ready to go?"

No one moved or spoke for what felt like ten minutes. Finally Jonesie took his helmet off and squinted so hard the veins in his forehead stood out. "You're gay?"

"Bi."

"And that's like mostly straight but kind of gay, right?"

"No. It's just bi," I replied, scanning the confused faces before refocusing on him. "It means I'm attracted to girls...and guys. But don't worry...not you. Any other questions?"

A tentative chuckle broke the strained vibe in the room. Then Jonesie shoved my chest when I raised my helmet over my head, immediately killing a return to normal. Blood rushed to my ears and through my limbs. I curled my fists and prepared to fight and maybe have the shit kicked out of me in the process. But I wasn't throwing the first punch.

"Have you always been bi? Like in every workout and every game? Or is it recent?"

I rolled my eyes. "Yeah, I've always been bi. You can't catch it, dummy. Don't worry. My cooties aren't gonna rub off on you. And believe it or not, I don't wanna rub off on you either. You're cute, but you're not my type."

Someone hooted with laughter and a few others joined in, but Jonesie didn't crack a smile. He looked confused as hell but not necessarily upset or disgusted.

"But the blond kid is your type. Is he your boyfriend?"

"He's the guy I'm crazy about. Leave him out of this," I hissed menacingly. "I'm still me. And I can still kick your fucking ass."

"Back off, di Angelo. I know who you are."

"You don't know me at all."

"Not true. I know you're one of us. That's all that counts." Jonesie smiled and held up his hand for a high five. "Score a few TDs for us tonight and I might just beg you to be my boyfriend too."

The room exploded in raucous cheer followed by a showtime rally cry. Christian grinned and inclined his head in what seemed like a nod of respect and acceptance before gesturing for us to follow him.

I RAN onto the field with my teammates, soaking in the frenzied atmosphere and the deafening roar of a sell-out crowd before taking my place behind Christian. The stadium was electric. Hypnotic even. It was only a glimmer of what I'd once dreamed of. But I didn't care about the crowds or the accolades now. Don't get me wrong, I wanted to win tonight. But I wanted something else too. Redemption, renewal...a chance to reclaim myself and start over again.

When the whistle blew, Christian faked a throw and passed me the ball. I barreled through our opponent's defensive line and ran forty yards. The ginormous guy who finally caught up with me bumped my shoulder hard when I stood and sneered. "Fuckin' faggot."

My initial reaction was to deck the motherfucker. I saw red...and then darker red. My nostrils flared as my adrenaline spiked. Some semblance of reason came over me before I did anything stupid. I pulled my mouth guard out and winked at him.

"This fuckin' faggot is about to score on your ass, dipshit. See if you can keep up." I blew him a kiss for good measure and jogged back to my team.

"What did you say to him?" Christian asked, furrowing his brow. "He's fuming."

"Good. It'll hurt a little more when we win. Keep passing me the ball. I've got this. I know what I'm doing."

And I did.

It was an epic game by anyone's standards. I scored three of our five touchdowns. The last one was my personal favorite. I leaped over a crouching opponent and ran into the end zone with five giants in hot pursuit. My teammates charged toward me with congratulatory shoves and high fives. And when the final whistle blew, I was surrounded.

This wasn't the LA Coliseum. We weren't Division One. Scouts weren't coming to see us play unless they had a kid on the field. When we graduated, we were going to get regular jobs like everyone else. But tonight, we were all-stars and we were heading for a championship. Students and friends and family members rushed the field as the local press pushed microphones in our faces. "We Are the Champions" blared in the background and lightbulbs flashed. It was surreal. Time stood still yet seemed to rush by at once.

I scanned the sea of humanity, frantically looking for Mitch. Chelsea said she'd bring him. No, she said she'd try. I didn't know what I was thinking, though. I didn't have a cell on me. There was no way to communicate—

I hurried over to our in-house announcer interviewing Christian and our coach. "Hey, can I use your microphone for a sec?"

The older gentleman who'd been calling local college games for the past twenty years flashed a grin at me. "You sure can! Congratulations on your amazing game, Evan!"

"Thank you, sir. Can everyone hear this?" I asked. A high-pitched buzz sounded when I tapped the mic. I swallowed hard and turned toward the stands. "Mitch, if you're here, I'm on the field at the end zone and...I'm out. All the way out. And there's a lot of people here so if you could just meet me at—"

"He's over there," Christian said, nudging my shoulder and gently taking the microphone back. "Go get him."

My heart threatened to burst at the sight of him standing in a halo of light next to Chelsea. He stood out in a crowd with his tight jeans and a sparkly "Rainbow crusader" sweatshirt. Or maybe it was something else entirely. All I knew was, he looked like sunshine. A sparkly, incandescent beautiful man. And fuck, I loved him. No doubt. I was L-word, all caps, head over heels for him.

I sidled through a small opening and raced toward him, pulling him into a fierce embrace. "You're here."

"You said it was important," he said against my chest.

"It is. I did it. I'm out."

"I heard." He stepped back and shot an indulgent smile my way and made a circular hand motion around the stadium. "Everyone heard."

"Good. I want everyone to know. I didn't mean to do it this way, but it feels...right."

"I'm happy for you, Ev," he said in a slightly distant tone. Then he bit his bottom lip and added, "If you ever need anything, you can call me or—"

"No. I don't need advice. I need you." I reached for his hand and pulled him close again.

"Evan, I think—"

"I love you. I'm done keeping it inside. I want everyone to know I'm crazy about you." I turned around and cupped my hands around my mouth and yelled at the top of my lungs, "I love this guy."

"What are you doing?" He laughed, his eyes crinkling at the corners. "People are looking at us."

"Let 'em look. Let 'em take pictures and post them on social media. Let them tag the wrong person and make up their own stories....None of that matters. We matter," I said, gesturing wildly between us. "Me and you. And I can't wait anymore. I can't let another second go by without telling you I think you're the best person on the planet. Let me be the one you lean on, baby. I'm not going anywhere. You're it for me. I love you, Mitch. And I'm pretty sure this is where you're supposed to tell me you love me too."

Mitch's openmouthed, shocked expression morphed into a wide, glorious grin. He nodded profusely and launched himself into my arms. He held on tightly before pulling back slightly to meet my gaze.

"I love you," he whispered, caressing my cheek and then sealing his lips over mine.

We ignored the catcalls and cheers, the flashing lights and celebratory music around us. It was a good night for beginnings and a perfect occasion to let go of the past. Somehow I knew the rough road of incredible loss and near death led me here. I wasn't sad about what was lost. I was grateful for what was found. Maybe I should have been scared as hell, but the sense of hope outweighed fear. The rest was up to us.

EPILOGUE

"I sn't it nice to think that tomorrow is a new day with no mistakes in it yet?"—L. M. Montgomery, *Anne of Green Gables*

THE SMELL of freshly mowed grass and roses wafted through the kitchen window. Someone was playing a Mariah Carey classic loudly. If the breeze wasn't a necessity on a warm summer day, I would have shut the window. Then again, maybe it was just me. It had to be. I plucked at the collar of my T-shirt and wished I had time to run home and change before Mitch arrived. Graduating from college and starting a new job seemed like a walk in the park compared to this. I was so nervous.

A knock on the front door ripped me from my reverie. I swallowed hard and hurried to answer it. I flung the door open wide and smiled at the beautiful man on the front porch and thrust a bouquet of pink flowers at him.

"What's this for, and where are we?"

"Flowers 'cause you like them and...well, come inside. No—wait."

I picked him up and carried him over the threshold. Not like a hero in a romance, though. More like a boyfriend who didn't want crushed roses on his new shirt.

"You're up to something. Spill it." Mitch pushed a stray lock of hair behind his ear and gave me a funny look. "I have class tonight."

He'd been busy with his internship at an LA-based marketing firm that primarily managed social media content for big companies. He hoped they'd hire him full-time within six months. According to Mitch, that would give him ample time to get acclimated to his classes in the masters program at UCLA. He was on the career path he'd envisioned before we'd graduated last month. And in a way, I was too.

Well, sort of.

I had no idea what my dream job was, but I was willing to give anything a try. Including real estate. I took my test before graduation and got my license right away. I was still in the process of building my clientele, but the market was hot so I figured I'd give it a try. This didn't have to be my forever job, but it was a good start.

Mitch was the forever part; the rest we'd make up along the way.

"Oh, yeah. Well, come on in," I said, pressing a quick kiss on his lips before pulling him down a short hallway to a spacious living room overlooking a good-sized backyard.

Mitch linked his fingers through my belt loop and narrowed his eyes. "Who lives here?"

"We do. If you want." I shrugged nonchalantly, as though my heart wasn't pounding in my chest.

He cocked his head and narrowed his gaze. "Keep talking."

"I think we should live together," I blurted. "I know it's a big step, but we're ready for this. Your studio is too small for both of us. And while I appreciate your grandmother's invitation for us to move into the main house...that ain't happening. Take a look. If you're not sold on it, we'll find something else. What do you think?"

"So you're asking me to live with you? Officially?" he asked with a sweet, shy smile.

"Yeah. Officially." I kissed his forehead and then his nose. "In a place of our own."

"Let's do it," he whispered.

"Don't you want to look at it? I have a few more I can show you in the neighborhood. This is just the closest to Maryanne and—"

"I love it." He swiped at his eyes and nodded.

"Hey, are you crying?"

"No. I'm...we're really doing this, aren't we? We're adulting and being responsible and—"

"Ugh." I made a face and shook my head. "I don't like those words. We're just being us and taking the next step. I'd ask you to marry me too, but I don't want to overwhelm you at once, ya know?"

Mitch threw his arms around my neck and beamed. "I'd marry you now, you know."

"Right this second?"

"Yes. I want to grow old with you, Evan. I want the whole next chapter and the fifty or more that come after that. I love you."

"I love you too, baby." I crashed my mouth over his and swayed him from side to side. When we finally broke for air, I kissed his hand in a chivalrous gesture and opened my arms wide. "Let me show you around. The yard is huge. Plenty of room for barbeques, handstand contests and best of all, we should be able to throw the football around easily."

Mitch groaned on cue and slipped his hand in mine. He moved to the sliding glass door and pulled me outside. Then he laid his head on my shoulder and flashed an adoring grin that told me he was with me all the way.

We didn't have to rush but we certainly weren't going to wait. Balance was the key. And with him at my side, our future was bright.

OUT IN OFFENSE - COMING JANUARY 2019

EXCERPT FROM OUT IN OFFENSE BY LANE HAYES (JANUARY 2019)

I placed my order then moved to the side counter to wait for our drinks... and respond to the email before I had to deal with a completely different kind of distraction. I snuck a peek at Rory and froze. His eyes were locked on me, like he was sizing me up and trying to figure me out. There was nothing overly personal or unprofessional in the look. Just curiosity. He smiled when he caught my gaze and suddenly, nothing seemed more important than being in the moment.

I stuffed my phone in my pocket, picked up our drinks and made my way back to the table.

"Here you go," I said, handing the latte to Rory.

"Thanks. Let's get this party started. Did you bring your last test?"

I unzipped my backpack, wincing as I slid the paper to him. "It was ugly."

He widened his eyes and let out a low whistle. "Damn. Do you at least get points for writing your name at the top?"

"Ha. Ha." I dropped my bag on the floor and sat down before adding, "I wish. I could use the extra credit."

"Hmm. Let's see your book."

I dug my textbook out and set it on the table then settled back in my chair to study him while he assessed the enormity of the challenge he'd taken on. His brow creased as he flipped through pages then glanced at the questions on my last quiz. I shifted in my seat hoping to clandestinely ease the pressure of my dick against my zipper. Call me crazy but the promise of being treated to nerd-speak from a badass former wrestler was the stuff of dreams. I sipped my iced coffee as I admired the intricate ink work on his arms and the script along his wrist. I leaned forward slightly to get a better glimpse, but it looked like it was written in another language.

"Do you speak Spanish?" I asked.

Rory did a double take then inclined his head. "A little. Do you?"

"No."

"All righty then," he replied with a half laugh before glancing down at the book again.

"Do you still wrestle? I mean, competitively?" Rory pushed the book to the middle of the table and grabbed his latte. He fixed me with a roguish stare and took a sip. Then he set the cup aside and leaned forward. "I thought we already did the 'get to know you' thing the other day. Do you really care if I wrestle anymore or are you stalling 'cause you think I'm gonna berate you for getting a crappy score on your test?"

I puffed up my cheek like a blowfish and nodded. "Yes."

Rory chuckled. "Okay, let's chat. I'm not here to make you feel bad about what you don't understand. I'm here to help. In normal everyday shit, I'm not known for my patience, but when I'm teaching, it's different. I'm fucking Ghandi here, you know? I want you to learn. So don't think I'm judging you. I'm not. I'm on your team. I'm not gonna spank you for getting a bad grade."

I licked my bottom lip and before I could stop myself, said, "That's strangely disappointing."

Rory opened his mouth and closed it theatrically. "You're flirtin' with me, Christian."

"No! No, of course not. I—"

I shook my head effusively and sucked on my straw until I gave myself an iced coffee brain freeze. I hoped when the feeling passed, I'd come up with the perfect one-liner to turn my awkward faux pas into a joke. I pushed my cup aside and gulped. Nope. I had nothing.

"You're not what you seem, are you?"

"Sure, I am. I'm a typical dumb jock. I can tell you anything you want to know about football, but don't ask me about Pythagoras' Theory," I said, elevating my dork status to tragic levels in a single blow.

Rory's eyes crinkled at the corners as he hooted with laughter. "Pythagoras' Theory? So what you're really saying is that you're a kinky ass geometry geek who happens to know how to throw a football. Good to know."

I crossed my arms and waited out a new round of merriment. "Are you finished?"

His shit-eating grin lit his eyes and made him look impossibly handsome in the boyish meets badass way that turned me inside out. This had disaster written all over it. If I couldn't get through fifteen minutes without making a fool of myself, I was in big trouble.

ABOUT THE AUTHOR

Lane Hayes is grateful to finally be doing what she loves best. Writing full-time! It's no secret Lane loves a good romance novel. An avid reader from an early age, she has always been drawn to well-told love story with beautifully written characters. These days she prefers the leading roles to both be men. Lane discovered the M/M genre a few years ago and was instantly hooked. Her debut novel was a 2013 Rainbow Award finalist and subsequent books have received Honorable Mentions, and were First Place winners in the 2016 and 2017 Rainbow Awards. She loves red wine, chocolate and travel (in no particular order). Lane lives in Southern California with her amazing husband in a newly empty nest.

*Be sure to join Lane's reading group, Lane's Lovers, on Facebook for immediate updates!

www.lanehayes.wordpress.com

ALSO BY LANE HAYES

Out in the Deep

Leaning Into Love

Leaning Into Always

Leaning Into the Fall

Leaning Into a Wish

Leaning Into Touch

Leaning Into the Look

Leaning Into Forever

A Kind of Truth

A Kind of Romance

A Kind of Honesty

A Kind of Home

Better Than Good

Better Than Chance

Better Than Friends

Better Than Safe

The Right Words

The Wrong Man

The Right Time

A Way with Words

A Way with You

Made in the
USA
Columbia, SC